D1480355

Pirates of Samarkand

Rita Ritchie

Pirates of
Samarkand

Illustrated by Robin Jacques

W·W· NORTON & COMPANY· INC·
New York

This book is for

JENNIFER REITCI

who wished for a mystery all her own.

Contents

1	THE STORM	11
2	RIVER ROAD TO SAMARKAND	25
3	PIRATES STRIKE AGAIN	39
4	HAWKS IN THE HILLS	49
5	STOLEN GOLD	59
6	A SPY AMONG FRIENDS	73
7	THE SECRET MESSENGER	85
8	IN PIRATE HANDS	99
9	ESCAPE TO DANGER	113
10	ISKANDER SETS A TRAP	125
11	THROUGH THE GATE	139
12	RIVER TREASURE	153

I

The Storm

The river flashed past, blue and silver in the spring sunshine, as the fishing boat approached the village of Takshan.

Haroun stepped over to the line controlling the sail and loosened it from its peg. His brother Nuri, two years younger, waited in the bow, ready to throw a mooring line to the men already on the riverbank. Haroun glanced back at the stern. His father, Iskander, stood by the tiller, his black beard and his turban both at a jaunty angle, for he was well pleased with their catch. Iskander nodded at Haroun. "Now!"

Haroun hauled the sail around. Iskander pushed the tiller smartly. The fishing boat turned in to the bank, nosing into the soft mud. Nuri cast loops of rope, which were caught by two other fishermen standing beside the river. Haroun and Nuri jumped over the side into the shallow water and helped pull the craft up on the bank among the other fishing boats. Haroun tied the line securely to their mooring post.

As they walked back, Nuri patted the slender pointed bow. "We have the best fishing boat on the River Zeravshan," he said.

Haroun laughed. "Today we certainly have the best catch. There are so many fish the boat can hardly hold them all."

Iskander's face appeared over the side. "More fish means more work. Sharpen your knives, my sons!"

They scrambled aboard the boat. Sitting down with baskets and knives at the cleaning board, they began to rapidly scale and clean the catch. Iskander carefully went over the nets, untangling the mesh and mending snags.

Haroun's knife flashed over each fish. The afternoon sun warmed his loose white trousers and tunic, but his white turban kept his head cool. Other men and boys, dressed as he and Nuri were, worked on the decks of the other beached fishing boats. A hard-beaten dirt path led up from the riverbank to the widely spaced houses of Takshan. Not far from the village well was Haroun's own house, square and flat-topped like all the others. His mother, Leilah, would be inside, preparing the meal, or perhaps in the garden, planting the first seed of the season.

A voice called from the bank. "Iskander! We need your advice."

Haroun and Nuri looked over the side at two other fishermen. Iskander joined his sons and called an invitation. "Come aboard then."

The men clambered over the railing. Their faces were serious. Haroun and Nuri bent to their cleaning, but kept their ears alert.

One of the men said, "We can't come to an agreement, Iskander. I was sailing home when I met Mahmud here, having trouble with his nets. They were so full of fish he couldn't lift them aboard and the strands were breaking. He called to me for help and I sent my son to him, the oldest, who is almost full grown. Together they brought the nets in, and Mahmud lost not a single fish, not a single net."

Mahmud began protesting. "I am an old man. My boat is small and I have no one to help me. Now he demands half my fish because Allah blessed him with strong sons! Is there no charity in his heart?"

Haroun glanced at Nuri and saw his younger brother make a face. Old Mahmud lived by himself in a far corner of the village. He was suspicious and secretive, always complaining that boys were after his garden and orchard. This wasn't true, for no one cared to go near his house. It had been dark and lonely for many years, Iskander said, ever since Mahmud's wife and baby son had died of fever on the same night. Mahmud's sorrow gradually changed into surliness. Haroun couldn't remember him ever having said a happy word.

Now Mahmud begrudged sharing his catch with the man who had helped him win it. The two stood before

Iskander, waiting for his decision. Haroun was proud that men brought their problems to his father.

Iskander began to speak, then broke off. "Look, here comes Sayyid Ad-Din down from his mosque. For many months we have been without a holy man to help us in our prayers and to teach our children and make judgments for us. Now that one has come to Takshan at last, let's show our respect by asking his advice in this matter."

Mahmud and the other man agreed and left Iskander's boat. Haroun watched Sayyid Ad-Din as the old gray-bearded scholar walked slowly and with great dignity in his fine turban and rich robes. The men went up to him, and they spoke together for some time. When they parted for their boats, Haroun couldn't tell from their expressions what the sayyid had decided. Nuri grinned mischievously. "Mahmud would look as sour parting with one fish as with a netful."

Haroun nodded, adding, "As for the other, a cheerful man is as content with a single fish as with a boatload."

"And I," said Iskander, sitting down with his own knife and basket, "am made cheerful by the sight of these fish on the drying racks. Let's hurry."

Haroun bent over his knife and made the scales fly.

When the cleaning was done, Haroun and Nuri lifted the great fish basket between them and made many trips to the drying racks in their yard. They rubbed the fish with salt and hung them to dry. The previous catch was already dried and carefully packed away in the fishing shed to await the cargo boats that would take their product to sell in the great cities, Bukhara downriver and Samarkand upstream.

Leilah came out of the house, holding something wrapped in a fresh white cloth. "Wash the salt from your hands, boys, and take this bread to Sayyid Ad-Din. It's newly baked."

Nuri sniffed happily at the cloth-wrapped loaf. "Will there be another for supper? Good! Then let's hurry back, Haroun, so we can eat it while it's still warm."

Together they went up the street of beaten earth that wound lazily among the houses with their large gardens and fruit trees. Reaching the main canal, cut from the river to the fields behind the village, they ran along the high earthen bank, in and out of the poplars flickering their new spring leaves. Smaller irrigation ditches led from the canal, and the boys jumped over these. Here and there men worked in the fields or the groves; and up on the hillside others herded sheep, for not all men of Takshan fished.

The ground began to rise, becoming steep fairly quickly. The canal with its network of ditches ended here. On the grassy slopes roamed sheep. Shrubbery began growing more thickly, gradually giving way to trees. The path divided. One branch held level across the face of the wooded hill, leading toward the mosque. The other climbed in zigzags up the steep tree-grown slopes. Haroun gestured at the surrounding woods. "If we have time, we can pick up some brush to take home for the fire."

When they reached the mosque garden, Sayyid Ad-Din was sitting beside the well. This was the first time in the two weeks since the sayyid's arrival that Haroun and Nuri had come to the mosque. The place had not changed at all in the many months it was empty and slowly crumbling into ruin. The roof of the minaret, a tall and slender tower, had fallen in and some of the steps inside were not safe. The mosque itself was scaling off at the sides, showing the raw brickwork under the once finely painted stucco. The little house where the scholar lived had a leaking roof, and its glass windows were broken. The garden well was still choked with brush, though some of it had been hacked away to make room for a waterjar on a rope. Beside the mossy curbstone of the well sat the old scholar, Sayyid Ad-Din, on a cushioned seat, holding a great book in his lap. Haroun and Nuri stood to one side, respectfully waiting to be noticed.

At the death of the former holy man, the villagers met and decided to send out letters asking for another scholar to settle among them to tend the mosque and teach the village children. No one in Takshan could write, and none had yet traveled to a large city where scribes could be hired. The task fell to Iskander. He had hailed one of the passing cargo boats and had journeyed upriver to Samarkand, the golden city. There he had letters written and sent out to the mosques of cities in every direction, across mountains and deserts. Later Iskander often recalled the wonders of rich, distant Samarkand while Takshan waited for a new holy man to come.

As the weeks, then months, went by without a reply, the villagers fell into the habit of asking Iskander to settle their disputes. Then one day a message came along the River Zeravshan that Sayyid Ad-Din would arrive in Takshan soon. The villagers rejoiced, even though when he arrived, two weeks before, the scholar proved to be a very old man, slow of movement and deliberate of speech. He didn't seem to mind the crumbling mosque or the overgrown garden. But he asked to be allowed to rest fully from his long and exhausting caravan and boat journey. He also needed time to decide what must be done to repair the mosque.

Now Haroun and Nuri stood before him with the new bread, waiting for the old scholar to look up from his book. Haroun thought that this scholar was not as frail as the former one, for though Sayyid Ad-Din's beard was gray, the flesh of his face and hands was firm instead of wrinkled.

The scholar raised his eyes. The boys stepped forward and offered the loaf. "Bread, effendi," said Haroun. And Nuri added, "Newly baked from our own oven!"

Sayyid Ad-Din gestured. "Set the loaf upon that stone, child, with my thanks."

Haroun did so, and then giving way to curiosity, he asked, "Effendi, what settlement did you make between Mahmud and the fisherman whose son helped him?"

The gray eyes flickered sharply. "Eh, you know of their dispute? But you are the sons of Iskander, are you not? He sent the men to me. I spoke thusly: take the fish Mahmud usually catches by himself and set that aside. Of the remainder, divide that equally between Mahmud and the man who helped him."

Haroun was impressed. "You have wisdom, effendi!"

Nuri said, "When we learn the Koran, perhaps we too will become wise. Is that the book you have on your lap? Read some of it to us, effendi!"

The sayyid's hands moved quickly to close the book. "Eh, I grow weary. Soon, perhaps, we will begin the school...."

Nuri asked eagerly, "What is the year? Will you tell us the calendar, effendi?"

Haroun pulled his brother's sleeve as a sign that he should not bother the sayyid. But the man was already answering.

"The year," said the old scholar ponderously, "is the five hundred and ninety-seventh since the Prophet Mohammed fled from Mecca, and the twelve hundred and eighteenth since the birth of the Prophet Christ. Now I think your mother will be looking for you both to attend the evening meal."

Haroun was embarrassed. "I'm sorry we interrupted your studies, effendi. Come on, Nuri."

The sun was very low, and it was too late to gather brush in the woods. They raced each other down the path and along the canal banks. They reached home just in time to help Iskander take the drying racks into the fishing shed, the larger of the two huts that stood in the yard. They would bring them out into the sun again the next day.

That night Haroun was roused from his sleep by the crash of thunder, a rising wind, and the pelting of rain. The wind tore down the valley of the Zeravshan until he could hear the peach trees whipping about in the garden. The rain grew until it lashed the flat rooftops and sluiced down from the overhang. Lightning flashed brightly outside the windows. Haroun saw Nuri stir in his blankets, but the younger boy did not awaken. Haroun lay back, and soon the sound of the pelting rain made him drowsy.

The next morning both boys jumped out of their blankets and splashed hastily in the washing basin.

Nuri said, "I dreamed of a great storm in my sleep, the last one of the rainy season."

Haroun rubbed his face dry. "There really was a storm, and it woke me up. Let's hurry out and see what the wind has done to our peach trees." Quickly they dressed in loose white trousers, short tunics belted by colorful waistbands, and soft-soled leather slippers. Winding on fresh white turbans, they pulled aside the curtain of their tiny sleeping room.

The kitchen was empty, for as usual the boys had risen before their parents. Outside, the first sunlight slanted between square houses and shone upon pools of rainwater.

"Some of the peach trees have branches twisted loose," said Haroun as they went through the orchard next to the garden. "But most are still sound, though this young one is uprooted."

"The seed Mother planted yesterday must have washed away," said Nuri. "Let's go see how high the river has risen."

They could hear the loud roaring of water before they came to the bank, slimy with mud. Brown with soil wrenched from the land, the current raced on, high out of its usual bed. Fishing boats that had been pulled well out on the water were afloat and tugging at their moorings.

Haroun pointed. "Nuri, our boat is missing!"

They ran to the place where they had beached the craft only the day before. The mooring post was bare of rope.

Nuri shouted, "Mahmud's boat is gone also!"

They quickly went from place to place along the bank and found that, altogether, four of the Takshan fishing boats had slipped their moorings. Haroun said, "I'll search downstream, and you go call Father at once, Nuri."

Nuri ran off, and Haroun began trudging along the bank, the hurrying waters roaring in his ears. There was a sandbank not far downstream where boats were often stranded if they worked loose from their moorings.

But when Haroun reached the spot his heart dropped. The sandbar was nearly covered by the racing brown current. There was no trace of the four fishing boats. Slowly he returned to the village.

Nuri was there with Iskander. Some of the other fishermen had also gathered, and others were hurrying down to the bank from their houses. Haroun told them there was no sign of the missing craft, and while the men talked of what to do, he idly traced a line of rain-swept footprints from the river to where they disappeared on the hard-packed earth of the village street. Apparently some fisherman had gone out near the end of the storm to make certain his boat was still safe. Whoever it was, Haroun envied the man able to return to sleep in the knowledge that his craft was secure.

The fishermen whose boats were still moored clambered aboard and set off to search for the other craft. There was nothing for the rest to do but wait for their return.

Iskander looked up the broad street. "Here comes Sayyid Ad-Din. Perhaps someone brought him word of our trouble."

The fishermen and the scholar met at the village well.

Sayyid Ad-Din pulled his gray beard in distress. "Alas, that you have lost your boats! But have faith that the best will come of this in time, my friends. Allah tests our courage thusly."

All day long the searching craft were away. When the sun was low in the sky the boats returned with the news that no trace had been sighted of the lost fishing vessels.

Iskander shook his head over the evening meal. "I can't understand it! Not a plank nor a torn sail has been found, and the men searched into the big irrigation canals, too. If we do not recover our boats, how shall we earn our living?"

For ten days the boats searched downriver but found nothing. At last the men had to give up looking and go back to their fishing. Those who had lost their boats gathered in Iskander's house to find a way out of their trouble. Sayyid Ad-Din was there, speaking words of encouragement. After some talk, Iskander said, "Our only hope is to find work in one of the big cities, save our money, and buy new fishing boats."

Mahmud, sitting off to one side by himself, grumbled loudly. "Bah, none of us will live that long. We will spend the rest of our days going from one menial task to another."

Iskander smiled. "I have a plan. We are six grown men and my two sons. We will look for work as a group. That way we can take on large tasks and earn more money than if each man found a small job."

Sayyid Ad-Din nodded. "If you must leave your homes, you can live together and share the costs."

"And if any of us falls ill, the others will do his work," said another of the fishermen. "When he is well, his job is still there."

The men liked the idea. Even Mahmud reluctantly thought it might work.

Iskander said, "Then it is agreed. Tomorrow we will hail a passing cargo boat to take us aboard."

Mahmud raised a question. "Upriver or down, Iskander?"

"We will go upriver," Iskander said, "to the city I have visited before—to Samarkand."

Haroun and Nuri looked at each other, and in spite of the misfortune that had brought this about, they grinned.

"Now we will see it for ourselves," whispered Haroun to his younger brother. "Samarkand—the golden city!"

2

River Road to Samarkand

The cargo boat Iskander hailed from the bank the next day was owned by a merchant in Bukhara who was sending licorice root, jars of oil, blocks of crude salt, and brass bowls to the markets of Samarkand. The freighter was double-ended like the smaller fishing boats, but it was much wider and had a broad flat deck to which the cargo was lashed. The great, square sail was hoisted on a single mast made of unhewn tree trunks, and it was controlled by ropes. The crew also used long poles to help the craft struggle upriver against the current.

Iskander and the captain of the boat soon agreed on the fare to Samarkand. The captain showed the Takshan men the big brass brazier in the bow, on which they could cook their meals, and allowed them to choose their own sleeping places amid the piles of cargo. Haroun and Nuri made a place for themselves beside the railing so they might see as much as possible.

As the big cargo boat worked back into the river current, the boys leaned over the side, shouting good-by to their mother, standing among the others along the bank. When a bend hid the village from sight, the boys changed to their everyday garments, folding up and putting away the fine trousers and tunics, newly made turbans, soft-soled beaded slippers, and their chapans, heavy robes worn over the other clothing.

During the three-day journey to Samarkand, Haroun and Nuri kept pointing out to each other the rich fields of wheat and rice, the thick groves of almonds, peaches, and mulberries. Canals led from the river, and waterwheels turned mills or lifted water into the irrigation ditches. Streams tumbled into the river, cold from their birth in the mountains that bordered the valley of the Zeravshan.

Villages along the river and fishing boats with their nets out greeted the cargo boat as it passed, shouting out the latest reports. The crewmen answered with the news their freighter had collected since leaving Bukhara. Some fields had been washed out by that bad storm more than a week ago. There was to be a great wedding next month. A new waterwheel was being readied to mill the winter wheat. A cargo boat just a day's sail behind this one had left Bukhara with a load of gold and silver goblets and a store of fine rare silks. These were to be taken by caravan from Samarkand to Tibet.

The River Zeravshan began dividing into many branches. Poling strenuously, the crew worked the freighter into first one branch, then another, choosing among the many streams and canals that threaded through the rich country.

Then, around a bend, appeared domes and minarets towering over high walls.

Iskander pointed. "My sons, that is Samarkand. The greatest riches in the world go through its gates, from the country of the Franks in the far west to the mighty lands of Cathay in the east."

The river led directly into the city. When the freighter passed through the entrance arch with lowered mast, Haroun and Nuri marveled at the thickness of the city walls.

Great and small canals led in every direction. As the cargo boat wound among grassy banks and under brick bridges, it passed flat-roofed houses with richly carved doors, some of them with slips leading from the canal so that boats could be brought inside. Sometimes streets followed the canal through which they poled, and Haroun and Nuri saw great numbers of bullock wagons, donkey carts, and even camel trains. Women, veiled in the city custom, grandly turbaned men, and, occasionally, roughly dressed nomads went about their business or dallied beside the garden pools or sat under the pomegranate trees, sipping apricot nectar.

The freighter swung into a broad canal where other cargo boats were moored along a stone embankment. The mooring basin was lined with warehouses, and the quay itself bore piles of goods waiting to be loaded.

Wearing their best clothes, the men of Takshan left the freighter. Iskander took them aside. "You have seen the work done by the men who sailed the cargo boat. I think we fishermen can do the same kind of work, and it will keep us all together. We can live in the boat, too, as they do."

One of the men said, "Perhaps we could even visit Takshan every time we passed."

Mahmud growled, "Not likely. We will have to let boys into our gardens to steal the apricots."

Iskander said, "I'd like to find work in one of the boats carrying gold and silver and other valuables. They say the pay is very high for the men who sail the treasure boats."

Mahmud gestured at a bale of licorice root nearby. "You will not find gold and silver here."

"There are other warehouse districts like this one throughout the city," Iskander explained patiently. "I've already asked the way to the merchants who deal in valuables."

They started through Samarkand's crowded streets, pulling aside to let a caravan from Herat through. At last they found the district Iskander sought and then asked their way to a merchant who dealt in gold and silver goods.

Inside the merchant's office it was shady and cool. The man listened to Iskander's request for work, then shook his head. "I'm sorry, but there are many men who want to work on freighters carrying valuables. The wages are high, for the men must be able to defend their cargo."

Iskander said, "Every one of us can give a good account of himself with the scimitar, effendi. Even my sons know how to handle the blade, as you know every boy must to become a man. We would have brought our weapons along had we known it would help secure work."

But the merchant still shook his head. "I do not doubt your ability to fight. But the high pay lures more men than there are jobs. If you want to wait, perhaps there will be places for some of you in three or four months. But if you need work now, I know of a man who must hire an entire crew for a new freighter he has just purchased." The man gave them directions to a merchant of textile goods.

On their way there, Mahmud grumbled, "It is as I said. We will spend our days walking the streets, looking for work!"

But Mahmud was wrong. The textile merchant was interested in hiring the entire group. "Are there seven of you? That is how many men I need."

Iskander said, "There are six grown men, but my two sons together do the work of a man."

The merchant shook his head. "I will not have boys in my boats. But I will hire you six men, and if I find one more by noon, you may sail today with your first cargo downriver to Bukhara."

They talked of wages and came to an agreement. Then Iskander spoke once more of Haroun and Nuri. "They are accustomed to working in a boat, and will prove useful."

"Perhaps," replied the merchant. "But two boys together can't lift as great a bale of wool as a man, nor as long a roll of finished carpet. Besides sailing, the crew must load and unload the cargo. You six may begin loading the new boat now."

There was nothing to do but agree. Haroun and Nuri

were deeply disappointed as they followed the Takshan men. Their new employer showed them the goods to be taken from his warehouse and then led them a short distance to the quay, where his boats were kept. He pointed out his new freighter. "One of you men must be the captain, and the others are to obey his orders."

Iskander nodded. "We will take turns being captain each trip."

But one of the men spoke up. "It is your advice we follow, Iskander. You shall be our captain."

The others quickly agreed, except for Mahmud. He only hunched his turbaned head into his chapan and said nothing.

When the textile merchant left his new crew to its work, Haroun touched Iskander's sleeve. "May we go to the great bazaar, Father? Perhaps Nuri and I can find work there."

Iskander frowned. "I don't want my sons to live and work alone in Samarkand while I am on the river. You will be of greater use at home in Takshan. You may visit the bazaar, but come back by noon." He counted out some small coins. "This is to buy something to eat."

Haroun carefully tucked the coins away in his cloth waistband. Then he and Nuri set off, following their father's directions.

As they went through the streets, Haroun said, "If Father won't let us work in Samarkand, Nuri, it will take him a long time to earn enough money to buy another fishing boat."

His younger brother nodded. "The others always worked two in a boat, and that is the way they'll save their money. But Father will have no one to help him."

Haroun added, "Neither will Mahmud, but—"

Nuri said quickly, "Nobody cares about Mahmud. He's mean and has no friends."

"It doesn't matter," Haroun went on. "Mahmud's boat was a small one, and he has no family to support. He'll be back fishing at nearly the same time as the others. Only Father will have to keep sailing up and down between Bukhara and Samarkand for a long time afterward."

They crossed a brick bridge over one of the canals, then turned to follow a series of reflecting pools bordered with jasmines and tulips.

Nuri asked hopefully, "Could we grow something at home to sell, as the farmers do?"

Haroun shook his head. "We have no land except our small garden. We have no sheep to herd either."

They went through some dark streets, roofed against the hot sun already climbing high in the sky. Suddenly they entered an immense square crowded with stalls, shops, people, carts, and animals. It was the great bazaar of Samarkand, where everything passing east or west met and changed hands.

Haroun and Nuri made their way among people dressed in strange clothes and speaking foreign tongues, as well as among men and women wearing the familiar turbans and chapans of their own land. They bought rice cakes for breakfast and a little bottle of pomegranate juice to slake their thirst. Then they watched the dyers working over steaming kettles, counted the hammer blows of the coppersmiths, and studied the magic fingers of the potters rapidly shaping vases and dishes. Men walked through the crowd, offering for sale colorful rugs, or peacocks, or lion cubs. In the middle of the square a camel caravan was forming. Not far away a cotton merchant led a string of donkeys. Then, shouldering its giant way through the crowds, came a caparisoned elephant.

Turning to watch the great beast, the boys stumbled on a beautiful carpet laid out on the ground. In the center sat a richly robed and turbaned man. Around him sat men of all ages and dress, putting questions to him, which he answered. Nuri whispered, "What is that man doing, Haroun? He's dressed like Sayyid Ad-Din."

Haroun said, "He's a scholar of the Koran. These men visiting the city are asking him the right thing to do for their problems."

The holy man was speaking of the Prophet's life when he saw the boys. He smiled and beckoned. "Come, sit close."

Men made way for them and they sat down on the carpet. The scholar asked them, "Where are you from?"

Haroun answered, "Takshan, effendi. It is on the river between Samarkand and Bukhara."

The holy man stroked his long white beard, then nodded. "I remember some months ago that letters were sent to all the mosques, asking for a scholar to go to Takshan."

Nuri spoke up. "And one did come, effendi! He is Sayyid Ad-Din, and he is very old."

The scholar's eyebrows rose. "Sayyid Ad-Din from Merv? But—that cannot be! I heard that Sayyid Ad-Din died of old age on the caravan journey from Merv."

Haroun shook his head. "There must be some mistake

in the names, effendi. Our Sayyid Ad-Din is old, but he has many years to live."

The holy man studied his folded hands a moment. "Yes, there must be a mistake. I would like to meet Sayyid Ad-Din and show him Samarkand's fine mosques. Tell him that, will you? He may stay with me, Sayyid Byram, and we will discourse on the Koran and other religious matters. And he can tell me of the doings in Merv."

Haroun rose from the carpet. "We will give him your invitation, effendi. He will surely want to come to Samarkand!"

Leaving the scholar the boys wandered around and looked at the stalls. Suddenly Nuri pulled at Haroun's tunic. "Look, there are hawks for sale!"

Together they went to the open-front stall. The hawk merchant was speaking with a customer. Haroun and Nuri gazed at the long poles running around the three walls of the booth. Perched on them were the hawks, every one with a leather hood over its head. Each bird was tethered to the pole by a leather strap around one ankle.

The merchant came toward Haroun and Nuri. "Don't get too close, boys, or the hawks will bate!"

Nuri whispered, "What does that mean?"

Haroun shook his head. Takshan men were not hawkers. Falconry was a sport for the very rich of the cities, or a way of hunting food for the very poor nomads of the plains and deserts.

The merchant explained. "Bating means to fly off the perch from fright or anger. The hawks are tethered, you

see, and if they bate they will fall head down. They can injure themselves badly that way."

Haroun asked, "Why is it that they let you come close?"

The merchant laughed. "They know me, and I know hawks! It is not hard to manage them if you learn their ways." He looked at the boys closely. "You have not come to buy or sell hawks, have you?"

Haroun shook his head. "We're only visiting, and must start back to our village at noon. I've seen hawks in the hills, but have never been this close to them."

Nuri said, "We were fishermen until the storm took our father's boat away. He has found work, but there was no place for us."

"You look like strong boys," said the merchant. "Perhaps I can give you work."

"Father won't allow us to stay in the city alone," said Haroun. "We must go back to Takshan and stay with Mother."

The merchant pulled his beard thoughtfully and muttered to himself, "Fishermen, eh? Hawks in the hills, you say." He spoke to Haroun. "There's a way for you to work for me. Do you think you could capture hawks in your hills and bring them to me to sell?"

Nuri's eyes widened with excitement, but Haroun replied slowly, "Effendi, we know nothing of catching hawks."

"You know what a net is," said the merchant. "An hour remains before noon. In that time I can tell you everything else you need to know."

It was a busy, often bewildering hour for Haroun and
Nuri. Between caring for his customers, the merchant
taught them the kinds of hawks and falcons in his shop,
showed them how to handle the birds, set them to work
repairing some old hawking gear to take along, and in-
structed them on the methods of trapping the birds of
prey. He told them something about how the hawks would
be trained and used in hunting. "But that is not your
concern. Most of my customers prefer to do their own
training."

Haroun glanced at the sky. "Effendi, it's nearly noon!
We must hurry back to our father and the boat."

Gathering their equipment, the boys thanked the merchant for his help, then hurried through the streets, over
bridges and along canals until they came to the quay
where the textile merchant kept his boats. Someone called
out, "Here they come, Iskander!"

Iskander walked toward them, a smile replacing his worried frown. "Ah, my sons! Hasten aboard, for we must set
sail at once."

The boat was piled high with bales of wool and cotton
and sacks of dyestuff. Haroun and Nuri settled themselves
out of the way as the men pushed the boat out into the
canal and began poling while Iskander stood at the tiller,
turning the big freighter from one waterway to another
until, at last, they were outside the walls of Samarkand.
Then the crewmen raised the tall mast and hoisted the
large square sail. Wind and current began speeding the
boat downriver.

Iskander walked back to where the boys sat beside a

railing. Behind him came a stranger. Iskander said to his sons, "This is Yussuf. He is of Samarkand, and he sails with us as the seventh crew member."

Yussuf's clothes were the rougher sort worn by poor people, and he seemed very thin, as if he had not had enough to eat. But his trim black beard and broad grin made him seem very cheerful in the face of bad luck. He said to the boys, "I hope you liked your visit to Samarkand. Perhaps you'll sail there often with us."

Iskander explained. "Our boat will pass Takshan once a week, and the merchant says we may stop to visit our homes. On each downriver stop, every second week, we may stay overnight."

Nuri exclaimed over the good news.

Haroun said, "Then we'll see you once a week, Father. Will Yussuf have a chance to visit his home in Samarkand?"

The new crewman shrugged. "I have no family, and this boat is all the home I need." He pointed to the pile of hawking gear beside the boys. "What have you there— equipment for hawking?"

Before Haroun could answer, a long hail echoed across the wide river from a fishing boat.

"Have you heard the news?" cried a fisherman. "A freighter carrying goblets of gold and silver and bolts of costly silks was attacked this morning!"

"Attacked!" The men in Iskander's freighter began talking excitedly. Iskander called out, "What happened?"

The fisherman told them that the freighter had moored along the river bank just one day's sail below Samarkand.

During the small hours of the morning pirates attacked, wounding and driving off the crew. They stole the cargo and set the freighter afire before escaping in their own, smaller, boats.

Nuri shivered in spite of his warm chapan. "Haroun, pirates on the River Zeravshan!"

Haroun answered, "Now I'm glad the Takshan men did not find work in a treasure boat!"

3

Pirates Strike Again

Aided by the current, the freighter's downriver journey to Takshan took only two days. When the cargo boat rounded the last bend before the village, Haroun saw that nearly everyone was waiting on the bank. News of their coming had been shouted up and down the River Zeravshan, and as the freighter moored beside the fishing boats, people congratulated the men for finding work. Sayyid Ad-Din was smiling. "You see, my friends, that good fortune follows on the heels of bad."

Haroun and Nuri were glad to see their mother after five days away from home. She embraced them, saying, "I'm happy my sons won't be on the cargo boat. I don't like being left all alone. Besides, now there's trouble on the river."

Iskander nodded. "Pirates attacked a boat carrying a precious cargo. But perhaps they will be content with their plunder and leave the river."

Sayyid Ad-Din asked, "Where do they come from, Iskander? Are these brigands from the desert, weary of attacking caravans?"

Iskander shook his head. "They say the pirates attacked in small boats. Perhaps they come from the mighty Oxus River to the far west. In times of flood, our own river spills into the Oxus, and tales of the rich cargo boats might have brought the pirates here. But if we're lucky, they'll take their stolen wealth back to where they come from and leave us alone."

Then Iskander introduced Yussuf to the villagers. Yussuf had stayed alone in the big cargo boat, and now, leaning over the railing, he waved his greetings to everyone.

The fishermen and the cargomen began strolling homeward with their families. Mahmud trudged off to his lonely house. Yussuf stayed in the boat. Haroun was going to ask him to come home with them when he saw a young servant woman holding a basket of food up to him.

Iskander called, "Haroun, come tell your mother of your plan to earn money."

But Haroun saw Sayyid Ad-Din making his slow patient way up the road toward the mosque. "I'll come in a moment, Father!" he called and he ran after the old scholar.

Catching up with Sayyid Ad-Din, Haroun greeted him. "In Samarkand, effendi, Nuri and I met a scholar in the bazaar. His name is Sayyid Byram. We told him all about you, and he wishes you to visit him."

Sayyid Ad-Din's eyes darted, and he seemed to grow paler. "What is this? But I cannot travel. I have not yet recovered from the long journey from Merv!" His hands trembled as he plucked at his long sleeves.

"You could go easily by boat, effendi! Father will stop at Takshan next week, and you could sail with him to Samarkand. The boat journey is very enjoyable, effendi!"

Sayyid Ad-Din muttered, "Perhaps boys enjoy such hardships, but it is different with an old man. No, no, I cannot go. . . ." He resumed his dignified pace toward the mosque on the slopes of the hills behind Takshan.

That night, Haroun, Nuri, and their parents feasted on lamb to celebrate Iskander's employment. But later in the evening they became quiet at the thought that Iskander would visit them only once a week. "In a year and a half," Iskander promised, "there will be enough money saved up to buy another fishing boat. Then I can be home always, and we will live as before."

"And Nuri and I can go back to working with you in the boat, Father," added Haroun. "But a year and a half seems a very long time."

Nuri spoke. "It won't take that long, Haroun. Soon we'll be selling hawks in Samarkand."

Iskander laughed. "First you must catch them."

Before dawn the cargo boatmen gathered on the riverbank. They said farewell to their families, and just as the first rays of the sun shone over the hills they pushed the freighter out into the current and raised the great square

sail. Soon the boat passed out of sight on its way downriver
to Bukhara.

Haroun and Nuri took their hawking equipment far up
into the hills among the tall larch and pine, where they
had often noticed hawks flying. They spent a long time
carefully setting net traps and snares in open areas of the
forest. Then, after eating the food they had brought, they
visited each trap again. Two had sprung but were empty.
Haroun saw what they had done wrong and fixed the traps
again. But no hawks approached any of their traps that
day.

After the evening meal at home, Haroun gathered mate-
rials for making decoys to lure hawks into his traps. His
mother, watching as she mended clothes, said, "I'm glad
you have something to keep you busy. But, Haroun, you
can't spend all your time in this new venture. There is
work to do in the garden and the house."

Haroun promised not to let their trapping interfere
with their regular tasks. Setting aside his decoys, he took
up a big clay jar and fetched water from the village well.

The next day Haroun and Nuri set the decoys on slender willow wands before each trap. The slightest breeze
made the wands tremble, and the decoys seemed like live
animals or birds. Haroun hoped this would lure hawks
into the snares. Then the two boys left the upper woods.

On the lower slopes of the hills they paused to gather
brushwood for their mother's cooking fire. With twigs
piled high in their arms, they walked slowly through the
sloping sheep pastures and the level fields to the village. As

they passed the first house a woman called to them. "What is this—the bushes are coming to Takshan!"

Haroun craned to see around his bundle of brush. An old woman was sitting under an apricot tree behind a house. She raised a skinny arm and pointed at Haroun. "Look, look! The bush has grown a head. Does it talk?"

Nuri's voice came from behind his pile of brush. "Haroun, I can't see anything but my feet."

"It is only old Zena. She thinks the bushes are walking." Haroun raised his voice to the woman. "It is only us, Zena. Haroun and Nuri with brushwood."

She had risen from her seat and was drawing back, afraid. Poor old Zena! She hardly knew the time of day or what was happening around her. Everyone was as kind as possible, often humoring her nonsense. She lived with her daughter and her husband. Both were busy all day long, the young husband in his fields and the daughter in the house. The old woman was harmless enough and was allowed to sit in the garden. They said she was "beloved of Allah," for only He knew what was going on in her poor confused mind.

Haroun didn't want her to be frightened, so he set down his pile of brush and went close. Nuri did the same. Haroun said, "You see it is only us, Zena. We gathered twigs in the woods."

She looked puzzled as she stepped forward. "In the hills? No one lives in the hills."

Haroun explained slowly and patiently that he and Nuri had gone to capture hawks, and that now they were taking brush home with them.

The old woman nodded many times. "Hawks, yes, I see hawks." She pointed to the sky. "I sit here and see them fly. I will help you, Haroun and Nuri. I will watch the hawks."

Nuri said, "You don't have to do that, Zena."

But Haroun muttered, "If it pleases her, let her do it." To Zena, he said, "That will be fine, Zena. You watch the hawks for us."

They left her mumbling to herself beneath the apricot tree.

Their mother was glad to see the brush they had gathered. When they told her about their meeting with Zena, she said, "Poor old woman! She is so close to the end of her days that already her mind has gone ahead of her. You did well to be kind to her."

They saw Zena again early the next morning as they started out to visit their traps. She called to them happily, "I watched the hawks for you, Haroun! Three of them flew above the hills."

"Thank you, Zena," he answered. They went along the canalbank, past the fields and groves, through the sheep pastures; when the path divided between the mosque along the wooded hillside and the forest above, they climbed into the hills.

One net trap had sprung but was empty; the imitation hare had been carried off. "I should have brought another decoy with me," Haroun said.

Nuri sighed. "There is too much to think of in trapping hawks. I'd rather go fishing."

"If we trap nothing at all this summer, we will never go

fishing," Haroun grumbled. He reset the trap but knew nothing would come of it until he replaced the missing lure. Most of their other traps were empty, but in the last clearing something fluttered and struggled in the loop snare.

Nuri began running. "A hawk, Haroun! We caught a hawk!"

The hawk was a shaheen, its black plumage flashing like jet in the early morning sun as it struggled on the ground against the cord looped snugly around its feet. Nuri bent down, bare hands ready to grasp the hawk, but Haroun pulled him back. "Be careful, Nuri! That beak and those claws can hurt you badly." He opened the sack he had taken along and drew on a pair of thick leather hawking gloves the merchant had given them. "Nuri, get the falcon sock ready."

Haroun seized the big dark hawk, carefully holding its powerful wings against its body with his gloved hands as Nuri slipped the open-ended sock over the bird, enclosing the shaheen snugly except for its head and feet. The hooked beak stabbed the air angrily until Haroun fitted on a leather hood so that the hawk could no longer see. Darkness helps keep hawks from fighting.

Haroun carefully cradled the bird, which was as long as Haroun's arm from shoulder to wrist. Then both boys hurried down the steep hills, running along the path where it was level, and at last reaching the fields. They jogged along the canalbank, eager to show their mother their first capture.

But house and garden were empty. Leilah was not at

home. Nuri said, "She will be at the well." They hurried between houses to the broad street in the middle of the village, where the well was located. But no one was there.

"Look," said Nuri, pointing to the river. "Everyone has gathered along the bank. Perhaps the Takshan cargo boat is coming!"

Haroun shook his head. "Not yet. Today the freighter is to arrive in Bukhara. Perhaps a fishing boat has stopped to give some news."

They reached the riverbank just as the villagers were starting to turn back to their houses, talking among themselves. Some shook their heads, and the faces of others seemed worried. Haroun and Nuri fell into step beside Leilah.

"See, Mother!" cried Nuri, pointing to the hawk Haroun held. "We've caught our first hawk!"

But Haroun saw that Leilah was troubled. "What's happened, Mother? Was the news bad?"

Leilah sighed. "There has been another pirate attack, Haroun. A boat from Bukhara, carrying uncut rubies dug from the mountains, peacock feathers, and ornaments of silver was attacked by night. The crew was driven off after many of the men were badly wounded. Two men were injured so severely that they will never be able to work again."

"What happened to the boat?"

"The pirates took it away with its rich cargo. Today pieces of it are washing up along the bank." Leilah put her hands to her face. "How terrible that such men have come to our valley!"

Haroun said, "Don't worry, Mother. Father's boat will always be safe, for it carries only ordinary things that the pirates don't want."

"I hope you're right, Haroun. But what would happen if the pirates made a mistake? They always seem to strike in the dark. Some night they may attack the wrong boat!"

4

Hawks in the Hills

As they walked back to their house, Haroun and Nuri talked about their hawk trapping, and by the time they reached their garden Leilah had become interested in their first captive. "Look at those shining black feathers! It's a beautiful bird, Haroun, but can you take care of such a large hawk?"

"The merchant told us how," Haroun answered. "The shaheen is well muscled, nearly full grown. It should fetch a good price in Samarkand."

Nuri asked, "Where can we keep the hawk, Mother?"

Leilah said quickly, "Not in the house! You may keep it in the garden shed if you take the things out of there and put them in the fishing shed."

They went to the smaller of the two sheds behind the house. Nuri sat in the shade of a peach tree and held the hawk in his lap, while Haroun emptied the shed and fastened a stout wooden pole along a wall inside for a perch.

Carefully setting the hawk on the pole, Haroun tied a leather thong to its ankle, fastening the other end to the perch. He took off the falcon sock, but let the hood remain. The shaheen stretched out its powerful wings, then put its hooded head down to investigate the tether around its ankle.

Nuri said, "When do we feed the hawk?"

"In three or four days," said Haroun. "The hawk will not take food until it knows it can't hunt for itself any more. Then we must feed it every day."

"I'll do that," offered Nuri. "I remember how the merchant showed us we must tie the meat to a wooden board and let the hawk peck food from it."

For the rest of the week they caught nothing, but then a half-grown saker got into one of the nets. So powerful was this hawk that it had almost torn its way free of the net when the boys found it. Two days later they caught three red shaheens, smaller than the black. All of these hawks were brought to the shed and kept tethered and hooded. Nuri spent a great deal of his free time catching mice and snakes, cutting up the meat, and tying it to the feeding board. Haroun made more decoys, constructed cages, and repaired traps in the hills.

Now many hawks began flying over Takshan, resting in the forested hills before resuming their flight. There was so much work to be done that two or three times Haroun and Nuri stayed in the hills overnight to be with their traps in the earliest dawn hours. Sometimes birds and hawks they did not want sprang the traps and had to be released. Often such unwanted captives tore nets and made off with the decoys.

Though they were busy, Haroun and Nuri were always home when the Takshan boat arrived for its visit of an hour or two on its way upstream and when it stayed overnight on its downstream journey. In this way they were able to tell their father every week how their hawk trapping was progressing.

The boys decided that Yussuf must have found a place for himself, because he no longer spent all his free time in the boat, though he still slept there, and ate the meals the serving woman brought from her farmer master. Once Haroun saw him walk slowly past Mahmud, who was weeding his garden silently and grimly. Yussuf greeted the old man casually and strolled on toward the fields in back of the village.

Iskander and the other men brought bad news from the river. The pirates were growing bolder, once striking two different freighters at two separate places on the river. People living along the banks and canals between Bukhara and Samarkand were becoming more afraid. "They will speak to no one they do not know," said Iskander. "Even we are careful when we spread river news. First we ask the villagers or the passing fishing boats if there are any strangers among them. If not, only then do we tell the latest reports. Eh, even for us cargo boatmen it is hard to come by news of boats carrying rich goods!"

Haroun was puzzled. "Then how do the pirates learn of

such boats, Father? They must be strangers on the river, and surely no one would tell them."

Iskander shook his head. "I know not, my son. Perhaps they hide along the riverbanks and listen to what is shouted between friends."

Leilah protested. "They can't be everywhere, Iskander! And yet it seems that only boats carrying valuables are attacked."

Nuri said darkly, "There must be a spy among the river people. He listens to everything, and then tells the pirates what he has heard."

Iskander and Leilah laughed.

But Haroun had the uneasy feeling that his younger brother might actually have guessed the truth.

A few days later, early morning mist swirled upward from the wet grass of the forest clearing as Haroun and Nuri walked toward one of their net traps. Something flickered in the tall grass, and the boys ran to it.

Haroun said excitedly, "It's another black shaheen, Nuri. And see what a fierce one it is!"

"Let me hold the hawk this time, Haroun," said Nuri.

Haroun shook his head. "You can handle a smaller hawk first, Nuri. But this shaheen is too powerful." He drew on the leather gloves and disentangled their prize from the torn net. "Now we have enough hawks to take to the merchant in Samarkand."

"But you must finish making that last cage," Nuri reminded him.

Visiting their other nets and snares, they found a small hawk caught in one trap. Nuri cried, "Let me handle it, Haroun! What kind is it?"

The hawk was not much longer than Haroun's forearm. Haroun looked at the slate gray back and tail, the brown wings and shoulders. "It's a kestrel, Nuri, good for hunting only mice and song birds. Let's set it free."

But Nuri protested. "The merchant said kestrels are for training boys in handling hawks. Let's take it to Samarkand to sell!"

Haroun shrugged. "All right, Nuri. But we won't get much money for it."

Nuri put on the leather gloves and carefully freed the friendly little hawk. He was able to pull on the falcon sock without help, and then he hooded the bird.

They started down the forested slopes, carrying their new captives. Haroun grumbled, "The kestrel will take up food and extra space. It's hardly worth taking to Samarkand."

But Nuri was already fond of the hawk he could handle himself. "I feed the hawks, Haroun, so it will be no trouble for you."

The morning sun was well up by the time they reached their house. They went through the garden to the shed where they kept the hawks.

Haroun opened the shed door. There was the whir of wings, the squawk of excited birds. Something dashed just over his head. "Nuri, Nuri, shut the door. The hawks are loose!"

Nuri slammed the door shut and huddled in one corner with their new captives while Haroun stumbled and dodged and cast his net. Only two of the hawks had gotten free, but they were the black shaheen and the powerful saker.

Haroun netted the black shaheen. "Look, Nuri, the tether is torn. Get me another strap." With the new tether Haroun leashed the shaheen back to its perch. Then he went after the saker.

The big, powerful bird dashed from ceiling to floor, and from wall to wall. Haroun was afraid it would ruin its long, stiff flight feathers. Finally he was able to get the net around the large reddish-brown bird. "This tether is frayed, too. Nuri, I think both hawks tore their leashes with their beaks. But why?"

Nuri hung his head. "Haroun, I—I forgot to feed them last night. I didn't remember until we were ready to sleep, and then I was too tired to come out here."

"What! Nuri, your laziness might have cost us two good hawks." Haroun tied the saker to the perch. The other birds were restlessly pulling at their leashes. One of the red shaheens pecked on the leather strap with his beak. "Yes, they are hungry. No wonder they're trying to eat through the leashes."

"I'll feed them at once." Nuri took up the feeding board and left the shed.

The next evening Haroun finished his last cage. Now he and Nuri would be able to take all their hawks safely to Samarkand when they boarded the Takshan boat tomorrow. Just as the last light was leaving the sky, Leilah asked Haroun to fetch water from the village well.

As Haroun left the house with the water jar, Nuri came out of the shed. He ran up to join his brother. "I fed the hawks their evening meal, Haroun. And I'll prepare their food for the journey."

At the village well they lowered the large drawing jar

into the water and pulled it up, spilling from the brim. Carefully balancing it on the well curb, Haroun poured water into the jar he had brought. Nuri gazed up the street. "There is Sayyid Ad-Din coming." When the scholar drew close, Nuri called to him, "Effendi, Haroun and I go to Samarkand tomorrow!"

Haroun added, "Do you have any errands you wish us to do for you there, effendi? We could see Sayyid Byram in the bazaar and explain that you cannot travel to visit him."

The old scholar coughed and cleared his throat. "Eh, perhaps I could travel after all." He thought a moment, then nodded briskly. "It would be fine to see Samarkand and to speak with a fellow scholar. Yes, Haroun, I, too, will come aboard your father's boat tomorrow."

The next morning Haroun and Nuri ate a hearty breakfast, then quickly set about their usual household tasks, while their mother readied their supplies for the journey. "Let's have everything ready when the boat comes," said Leilah. "Then we can spend that hour or two visiting instead of working."

Suddenly Haroun remembered the traps and snares in the forested hills. "Nuri, I must spring the traps and snares so no hawks are caught while we're gone. Otherwise they'll injure themselves trying to escape."

"Hurry, then, Haroun. I'll finish your work here."

Haroun ran through the village. As he passed the last house, old Zena called out to him. It was something about a hawk, but Haroun had no time to stop. "Yes, Zena, thank you!" he shouted and ran on.

He climbed the path up the wooded slope, pausing at

the fork to catch his breath. Here the side path turned off toward the mosque. Sayyid Ad-Din still had not held any classes, but he was said to be busy repairing the mosque and the tall, slender minaret. The minaret needed a new roof, and Haroun wondered how Sayyid Ad-Din would fix it, for the scholar had not yet asked anyone to help him.

Climbing into the hills, Haroun sprang the traps, releasing a raven and a lark. Hiding the decoys under bushes, he returned to the village as quickly as he could.

He met his mother coming out of the house. "Nuri has gone ahead to the river," she told him. "The boat is around the bend."

Together they went to the riverbank. Other families were there as were the fishermen, delaying their own work in order to visit with their friends from the cargo boat. The midmorning sun glared on the hard earth, for spring had turned to summer, and the days were growing hotter. Already the rains had stopped for the season, and the river was beginning to drop. In the weeks ahead everything would get drier and dustier; only the canals and irrigation ditches, filled by the waterwheels, would keep the gardens and groves lush and growing.

"Here comes the boat!" cried Nuri, pointing downstream.

The big double-ended freighter struggled around the bend against the current. The wind helped, pulling on the great square sail. The deck was piled high with the familiar bolts of plain rough cloth, rolls of carpeting, piles of common rugs, and bundles of ordinary chapans and turban cloths.

Amid shouts of greeting from the villagers, the crew swung the sail and dug in with the long poles. The boat fought its way out of the current into the calmer water near the bank. Fishermen caught the mooring lines, slipping them over the stakes driven into the ground.

The crewmen climbed out of the freighter. Their faces were grim, and they strode like angry men.

Iskander spoke even before he reached his family. "Last night the pirates struck a boat moored but an hour's sail from us. We are fortunate they did not attack our boat by mistake. From now on we are taking our scimitars with us!"

5

Stolen Gold

The two-hour visit passed quickly. Haroun and Nuri walked back to the moored freighter with their father and mother. Besides their bundle of provisions, each boy carried two large hawk cages. They put everything aboard the cargo boat, and Haroun arranged a cloth over the cages to shelter the hawks from the hot sun.

The other crewmen and their families came. Iskander gazed at the mosque behind the village. "Nuri, are you certain you gave Sayyid Ad-Din the message as I told it to you?"

"Yes, Father. He said he would come, but he is old and walks slowly."

"Here he comes now," said Haroun.

The boatmen went aboard the freighter and made ready for casting off. Each had brought his scimitar with him, laying the weapon in a handy place. Yussuf had no scimitar, but Iskander had brought an extra one, for he owned two fine blades. Haroun and Nuri had wanted to bring their own smaller weapons along, but Iskander had told them that only the crew were to fight.

Sayyid Ad-Din finally reached the riverbank. Two fishermen swung him up to the freighter's railing, and Mahmud and Yussuf helped him into the boat.

Mooring lines spun through the air, the sail swelled in the wind, the tiller swung, and the big cargo boat edged into the current. Haroun and Nuri shouted farewell to Leilah.

The three days of the journey passed quickly for the boys, since they were allowed to help work the great sail or hold the tiller. Though they were useful, Mahmud managed to find fault with them, and they avoided him as much as they could. They busied themselves caring for their hawks, keeping them fed and watered, and sheltering them against the heat. Yussuf had taken on the job of cooking, and the boys worked with him. They saw little of Sayyid Ad-Din, who spoke seldom and kept to himself. Haroun supposed that the scholar was meditating on the coming discussions with Sayyid Byram.

At last the walls and towers of Samarkand rose in the distance. Finding its way through the maze of streams and canals, the freighter entered the city and quickly threaded through the many waterways to its own quay.

Sayyid Ad-Din thanked Iskander for passage to the city.

"I will stay with Sayyid Byram for the night. Do you start downriver tomorrow morning?"

"Yes, effendi," replied Iskander. "But come early, for we leave an hour after dawn."

Sayyid Ad-Din went his way, while Haroun and Nuri carefully picked up their hawk cages and set out for the bazaar. "We mustn't excite the birds," said Haroun, "or they will break their flight feathers and become worthless."

It took them a long time to reach the great bazaar, for they stepped aside to let every person and animal pass by so that their cages would not be jostled. At last they arrived at the huge crowded square. The hawk merchant was glad to see them. "A saker!" he exclaimed. "And these two black shaheens are indeed fine ones. But why did you bother with this kestrel?" Then seeing Nuri's disappointment, the merchant added, "The kestrel is a very good one, but remember that the larger hawks bring the most money." He began to leash the big saker to one of the long bar perches. "Will you sell me your cages, too? They are roughly made, but good enough for a customer to take his hawk home in."

"You may take the cages, effendi," said Haroun, glad to turn this burden into an extra coin or two.

"Good." The merchant opened the leather bag hanging at his waist and counted out their money. "And here is some scrap leather you may use, if you have to make more hoods."

Haroun and Nuri stayed with the merchant for some time, helping him and learning more about hawks. The rest of the day they spent wandering around the immense bazaar, watching leather workers, jade carvers, glass blowers, and jugglers. Sometimes they let themselves be carried along by the thick traffic of camel trains, donkey strings, and bullock carts driven or ridden by people in fine town clothes, the rougher dress of country, or the strange garments of faraway lands.

At noon they ate the cold boiled rice Haroun had carried along from the boat. Nuri sniffed the lamb broiling over charcoal, and stared hungrily at the piles of sweets on trays. "Haroun, can't we buy anything to eat?"

Haroun shook his head, though his mouth watered at the sight of these delicacies. "We must save every coin for our fishing boat. Father says it will take much longer than he thought to put enough money aside."

When it was time to go back to the cargo boat late that afternoon, Haroun thought he could find a shorter way. "The usual way takes us past a blue-tiled alley archway near the bazaar, Nuri. If we take the alley straight through, we should come out near that large canal bridge we must cross to reach the textile-warehouse section. Let's try it!"

Haroun led the way through crowded, winding streets and soon found the alley entrance-arch faced with blue tile.

Nuri pulled back. "It's dark in there, Haroun."

"I see daylight between those buildings. Come along."

Haroun went first. The alley led to a courtyard with many tiny streets leading from it. Haroun chose one, and they went through it, but it curved back and he had to find another leading in the direction he wanted to go. Before long Haroun realized they were lost in a tangle of winding and turning streets. They had passed only two or three persons since they had entered the blue-tiled archway, for in this section there were only houses with but an occasional quiet shop. At last they found a woman drawing water from a well in one of the many small courtyards. Haroun asked her the way.

"You must go back through the blue-tiled arch," said the veiled woman. "All streets in this section lead to the alley by which you came." She gave them directions.

Thanking her, they retraced their steps in the fading daylight. They came out under the blue-tiled arch and took the familiar long way back to the quay.

Yussuf joked with them as they ate a late supper in the boat, now filled with goods to take to Bukhara. "You must have had a hard time deciding how to spend all your money, or you would not be late coming back."

"We spent nothing, Yussuf," said Haroun. "What we earned from selling the hawks must be saved for our fishing boat."

Yussuf nodded approvingly. "That is a fine idea, but you should have some reward for your hard work. When I was a boy, my friends and I used to wade in the canals to find jade to sell."

Nuri shouted with excitement. "Jade—in the canals?"

Yussuf nodded. "Though it was not very good jade, it brought a few coins our way. Eh, it is too bad we must leave shortly after dawn tomorrow."

Haroun glanced at Nuri and muttered, "That leaves us a whole hour for hunting!"

The last of the sunset drained out of the sky. Men were

dark shapes against the red glow of the coals in the brazier
as they prepared for sleep in the boat. Yussuf took up his
ragged chapan to use for a blanket, and went to his accustomed place.

Haroun and Nuri hurriedly washed and dried their
bowls, then unrolled their blankets.

Nuri whispered, "I wonder why Yussuf spends the night
in the boat. Was he not born in Samarkand?"

"Yes," muttered Haroun. "But he says he has traveled a
good deal and now he finds there are no friends or relatives
left in the city."

It did seem odd that Yussuf did not talk of his past. But
he was a cheerful worker and got along well with the others. Even Mahmud had ceased complaining about the
stranger when Yussuf, ignoring his grumbling, treated him
no differently from the rest of the Takshan men. This did
not keep Mahmud from his usual surliness, and except for
Yussuf and Iskander, everyone else kept away from him.

When Haroun and Nuri awoke, the night sky was
faintly blue with the coming dawn. Putting on chapans
against the chill, they breakfasted on the crusty bread
Haroun had set aside from his supper. The crewmen slept
on, dark figures huddled here and there among the bales of
cargo.

Nuri whispered, "Where shall we look for the jade?"

"Not here in the mooring basin," replied Haroun.
"There is no place to wade among all these freighters.
Let's go to the big bridge we cross on the way to the
bazaar."

Quietly making their way between cargo and sleeping
men, they reached the stone quay. The faintest gray light

from the sky above guided them through empty brick-paved streets, past barred doors and deserted courtyards. It was a little lighter when they reached the bridge. Taking off their soft-soled slippers, they put them in their waist-bands for safekeeping. Then they rolled up their trousers and waded into the cold water.

The canal surface glittered here and there with the brightness of the growing dawn. Haroun felt the fine silt with his bare toes. There was someting hard, but when he picked it up with his hand it was only a stone. The boys kept on searching, moving farther along the canal. "We can wade all the way to the edge of the bazaar," said Haroun. "Then we'll go back to the freighter through the usual streets."

Nuri waded and splashed about eagerly, but Haroun hunted more carefully. Yet it was his younger brother who found the first piece of jade, a little yellow chip. Soon after, Haroun discovered a large smooth jade pebble. Then they both searched quietly and intently, working farther along the canal. The water was like a sheet of silver in the new day.

"Haroun, come here!" came Nuri's call from ahead, soft but urgent. He had reached a place where willows grew thickly from the wall of a house straight across the bank to the water's edge.

When Haroun joined him, Nuri was digging with his fingers in the muddy canal bank next to the willows. Something flashed in the early morning light. "What's this?" Nuri asked. "It was in the mud right here out of the water."

Haroun took it and scraped away the mud. It was a

round piece of bright-yellow metal. On one side was stamped a star within a star. The other side, curiously, was blank. "Nuri, this—"

Suddenly chains rattled and something heavy began rumbling. When it stopped, a voice came from behind the thick willow growth. "You must hurry! The sun has already risen!"

Haroun, startled, dropped the metal disk. He looked around, but there was nothing to be seen through the dense willow growth. The voice continued. "I have had no rest this whole night with our talking and planning."

A new voice came from behind the shrubs. "We thought it best to bring you these valuable things at once so that you can send them over the mountains without delay."

"My caravan must travel secretly, for most goods cannot be melted down like those things you brought last night. Eh, they must wait, for you keep my furnace too busy!"

Water swirled and wood knocked on wood as if a boat were being poled away. There was a muttering, and then the first voice said, "What, you want to go along? No, it's dangerous to be seen in the boat with them. You other men, go, but remember the new signal."

The other voice, which seemed to belong to the boat, said, "Two quick pulls of the bell, then one more. Farewell, both of you." Water swished more rapidly as the rhythm of poling increased.

Haroun expected the boat to pass him and Nuri as they crouched beside the willows. Instead the sound of swirling water faded away.

Behind the willows the first voice spoke again. "Go through the streets as if you were on some early errand."

Again the person with him muttered. He must have been the second man to whom the voice in the boat had bade farewell. The first voice said in reply, "No one will know you have left this house. All streets in this section lead toward a single blue-tiled archway near the bazaar. Come, I will set you on your way."

Once more a rumbling came from beyond the willows, followed by the muffled clink of chains.

In the morning stillness Nuri whispered, "What were those men doing?"

"They must be merchants," Haroun said. "You know that many traders keep their sources and markets a secret. Even craftsmen guard jealously many of their methods." He glanced up at the sky, now fully lighted by the sun. "We must hurry, too, for Father's boat will soon set off downriver."

"What about the piece of jade I found?"

"It wasn't jade," said Haroun. He searched around on the muddy bank. "Here, Nuri, it's some kind of gold coin. Look, is that a footprint?" Haroun's fingers traced the outline of a slippered foot in the mud. Where the ball of the foot should have made a smooth hollow under the weight of the owner, there was, instead, a curious wedge-shaped indentation. It was as if a bone had been broken and had mended without being set in place. There were other footprints trampled in the mud near the water, but only a few had the peculiar dent.

Nuri said, "I saw marks like that when I found the coin. Somebody had pushed it into the mud."

Haroun frowned. "These marks seem familiar. If only I could remember!"

"We don't know anyone in Samarkand," Nuri reminded him.

The crooked footprints led close to the wall of the house, where Haroun found a break in the willow growth. The boys went through. A few steps along the wall took them to a thick wooden door. The canal bank was cut away so that the water lapped against the solid iron-bound planking. Haroun whispered, "That's the water gate that was pulled up to let the boat out." An iron ring hung from a rope leading through a hole high in the wooden gate. "That must be the bell to signal arrival, as the merchant said," muttered Haroun.

Quietly he led the way through the water and up the farther bank. Ahead the canal curved out of sight. Haroun did not speak again until they were well past the water gate of the merchant's house. "If we take the next path away from the canal, we should come out at the bazaar."

"Why did we have to be so quiet back there?" asked Nuri.

"If the merchant had come out and questioned us, we might have missed taking Father's boat homeward."

Here the bank was higher and dry. They wiped their feet with bunches of grass, then put on their slippers.

Turning onto the next street leading up from the canal, they came to the huge bazaar. Haroun and Nuri skirted the vast open place with its deserted stalls and shuttered shops, and then began a steady jogging run along the familiar way back.

As Haroun rounded a corner he suddenly ran into a man coming out into the street. "Here, be careful!" exclaimed the man, stumbling back against the wall.

Haroun stopped. "Why, it is you, Yussuf!" He righted his tilted turban, and Yussuf smoothed his own garments. In the dim light of the narrow street Haroun saw a bright golden flash that Yussuf quickly tucked out of sight in his waistband.

The boatman said a little sharply, "What are you boys doing in the streets at this early hour?"

"We're looking for jade," Haroun answered.

Nuri pulled his jade stones from his waistband. "See what I found, Yussuf!"

While Yussuf examined Nuri's find, Haroun noticed that behind the man there was an alley archway faced with blue tile. Yussuf had been coming out of there when Haroun bumped into him. This was the single passage that led to the maze of streets, courtyards, and houses where Haroun and Nuri had become lost only the day before. Somewhere in this labyrinth stood the house on the canal through whose water gate a boat had secretly left not long ago.

Yussuf returned Nuri's stones. "They are worth a little something, but you must wait until your next visit to Samarkand to sell them. Have you had your breakfast? Then let's go back to the boat."

They hurried back to the quay, Yussuf occasionally stumbling on the cobblestones. "I'm no longer accustomed to dry land," he said with a laugh.

When they reached the freighter, they found the crew already wide awake. Yussuf went aboard and, bending over the charcoal brazier, kindled a blaze for cooking the rice. Iskander called out, "You are an early riser, Yussuf."

The cheerful boatman replied, "It is the only time left for a busy cargoman to go visiting."

Haroun and Nuri began helping Yussuf with the cooking. "Will Sayyid Ad-Din eat with us? asked Haroun. "Perhaps Sayyid Byram will give him his breakfast."

"Here comes Sayyid Ad-Din now," said Yussuf.

With his usual dignity, Sayyid Ad-Din paced slowly across the broad quay toward the boat.

"Look behind him," said Nuri. "There is Mahmud walking with a stranger."

The two men had their turbaned heads together. When Mahmud saw the boatmen at the breakfast fire he left his companion and hurried across the quay. He reached the freighter at the same time as Sayyid Ad-Din. Mahmud said to him, "Salaam, effendi. Let me help you." And taking the old scholar's arm Mahmud assisted him into the boat.

When Mahmud joined the men awaiting their breakfast, Iskander said in mild reproof, "It is well you returned now, for we sail within a quarter hour. Did you hear any news in the bazaar?"

"The bazaar is empty at this hour," Mahmud said sulkily, "except for this one man, a stranger whom I met by arrangement, for last night he promised me riches. Bah! He would have me sell my life or limbs in a boat carrying valuables to Bukhara. True, the wages are doubled now, but it would be my luck to meet the pirates even though the man promised the boat would leave the city in secret. And now, Iskander, you know as much about my business as I do." He growled at Nuri, "Bring me my rice when it is ready." And old Mahmud stamped down the length of the boat to the stern.

Iskander ignored Mahmud's rudeness. "If wages on the treasure boats have doubled, this is something for us to think about."

"Not I, Iskander," said Yussuf firmly, ladling Mahmud's rice into the bowl Nuri held. "I do not fear a fight, but neither will I risk myself against such odds."

"Perhaps cleverness is a better weapon than a scimitar," replied Iskander.

A half hour later the freighter had wound its way through the canals of Samarkand and was passing beneath the thick city walls. The first fishing boat they met shouted the news. "Pirates attacked again last night! Crew driven off and all the cargo stolen from a boat going downriver from Samarkand."

Iskander called over the broad river. "What was taken?"

"Bolts of silk, rare spices, and sacks of gold ornaments to be used for mounting on weapons and saddles. The ornaments were like coins, stamped with a star within a star, the other side blank."

Haroun and Nuri stared at each other. The "coin" Nuri had found near the Samarkand merchant's water gate was really a gold ornament exactly like the kind stolen by the pirates!

6

A Spy Among Friends

As the cargo boat moved swiftly downriver from Samarkand, Haroun and Nuri crouched inside a cave they had built of cotton bales. There was just enough space between the bales to let in air and some daylight, but not enough to allow their words to escape.

Haroun turned over in his fingers the gold disk Nuri had found beside the canal early that morning. "Yes, it's the same as those ornaments stolen by the pirates. Here's the star within a star, and the other side is blank. A real coin would have a design on both sides. The fisherman said all these decorations were made in one lot, for sale, and there are no others like them."

Nuri was puzzled. "But how did this get beside the merchant's water gate in Samarkand?"

"It could have been dropped by one of the pirates." Haroun felt excitement rising. "Think of it, Nuri, the pirates themselves coming to Samarkand! It would be easier for them to hide in the great city than in any of the villages along the river, where everyone knows everyone else."

Nuri stirred restlessly in the little cotton-bale cave. "That means the merchant himself must be a member of the pirate gang, Haroun. After they attacked the freighter last night, they carried their treasure to his house. One of these gold disks fell to the ground, but no one noticed."

Haroun nodded. "And one of the pirates stepped on it, one with a broken foot." There was something about that footprint that bothered Haroun. Trapping hawks in the hills of Takshan had taught him how to read little signs in the grass, the mud, the bushes. Now the crooked footprint was trying to tell him something.

Nuri went on. "I found the gold disk just before the water gate opened, and the men came out to sail away. How I wish we'd looked beyond the willows! Why, Haroun, we would have seen the pirates themselves."

"We might have been caught by them too!"

"There was just one boat, Haroun," said Nuri. "I could tell by the sounds. Only some of the pirates came to Samarkand, and they soon left."

Haroun said thoughtfully, "It's a five- or six-day sail between Samarkand and Bukhara. And treasure boats have been attacked all up and down the river. Then the pirates must really be hiding somewhere else, Nuri, and not in the golden city itself."

His brother nodded. "Perhaps they hide only their plunder in Samarkand. Then they sail back to their secret place to await word of another boat loaded with riches."

Haroun wrinkled his brow. "How would they learn of such boats? No one speaks to strangers any more. Even if the merchant with whom they hide their stolen riches should hear talk in the bazaar or on the quays, here he sits in Samarkand, while they lie hidden in their boats somewhere along the river, days away."

"They have a spy working for them," Nuri declared. "I said that long ago, but Father only laughed. Someone listens for the pirates and goes to them with the news."

"The crooked footprints!" A sudden idea flashed through Haroun's mind. "The crooked footprints were mingled with some others on the muddy canal bank, Nuri. But there was also a separate line of them leading along the wall of the house to the water gate. Whoever made those prints was not with the pirates when they brought their latest stolen riches to the merchant's house. Crooked Footprint came alone, and he came after the pirates did because he stepped on the gold disk that had been dropped."

Nodding, Nuri added, "I had to dig it out of the mud where the foot had pressed it in. Crooked Footprint must be the pirate spy, Haroun, come to fetch his share of the wealth."

"He is not of Samarkand," Haroun said. "Remember how the merchant spoke to someone who wanted to leave in the boat with the pirates? That must have been Crooked Footprint, and he must have come in the night, sneaking in by the water gate. The merchant told him how to go through the streets, for they all led to that blue-tiled archway near the bazaar."

Nuri cocked his head thoughtfully. "Is that the archway where we got lost yesterday and where we met Yussuf this morning?" When Haroun nodded, Nuri said excitedly, "Perhaps Yussuf saw Crooked Footprint! Oh, Haroun, let's ask him."

Nuri rose to leave their secret place within the cotton bales. But Haroun put a hand on his arm. "Wait, Nuri. You forget that Yussuf himself was coming out of that alley when I ran into him. And he—he had something gold hidden in his waistband. He covered it hastily."

"Yussuf—a pirate spy? No, Haroun, you are wrong! Why, other men were abroad in the streets at that hour. There was Sayyid Ad-Din, and Mahmud, too, walking with a stranger. Anyone could have come out of the archway after we left with Yussuf."

"Whoever it may be was in the merchant's house before we came along looking for jade. Nuri, when we left the freighter at dawn, did you notice if any of the crew had left before us?"

His younger brother shook his head. "All I remember seeing were mounds of blankets. I was afraid someone would waken and tell us not to leave the boat." He thought for a moment. "Haroun, Mahmud has gold on him, too. I saw it as I brought him his breakfast rice. When he reached for his bowl, the folds of his chapan parted, and

I saw something gold, a disk, hanging about his neck. He jerked his robe shut and growled at me to stop staring and let him eat his rice. Perhaps that gold was his pay for the latest pirate attack. He could have gotten it from that stranger he was talking to this morning."

"I don't care for Mahmud, either, Nuri, but that doesn't make him a pirate spy. How would he ever meet the pirates in the first place? Besides, no Takshan man wants this danger to remain in the river valley."

"Mahmud always fished alone," said Nuri. "Who can say when and how he met the pirates? And anyway, he isn't really a Takshan man at all. No one knows where he comes from."

Haroun nodded in reluctant agreement. He remembered his father telling how Mahmud had come to Takshan from a passing caravan with his wife and baby son after he had suffered some accident to his foot. When his foot had healed he decided to stay and become a fisherman. It was several months later that his wife and son died of fever. The little family had always kept to itself, and after the burials Mahmud became more secluded than ever. The passing years turned him bitter and self-centered.

Haroun said, "Yussuf is not a Takshan man, either, Nuri. He's cheerful and friendly enough, but he doesn't even have a home in Samarkand, where he says he grew up. He could actually be a stranger in the city, knowing no more than we do of its streets and alleys."

"But the pirates were already attacking cargo boats before Yussuf joined the crew," Nuri objected.

"They must have known that soon people would stop

trading river news with passing strangers," said Haroun. "So they sent one of their band to get a job and spy out the information needed." The more Haroun thought of it, the more likely it seemed. "That must be the way news of the cargo boats reaches the pirates so quickly. Yussuf has only to steal away some night when the boat is tied up at the bank near the pirate hideout."

Nuri's chin lifted stubbornly. "If anyone is a pirate spy, Haroun, it's Mahmud. We must watch carefully to see if he limps."

"If he—Nuri, what do you mean?"

"A crooked footprint means a broken foot that didn't heal the right way. If the pirate spy walks with a limp, it will be easier to find out who he is."

Haroun said firmly, "Mahmud doesn't limp. I'm certain of that."

Nuri said, "Yussuf doesn't limp, either."

Haroun agreed. But he couldn't help thinking how easily Yussuf had stumbled on the cobblestones when he walked back to the boat with them that morning.

When the freighter reached Takshan two days later, the villagers quickly gathered along the bank to welcome the crew. They exchanged the recent river news, and spoke fearfully of the latest pirate attack. The wives of the cargomen didn't want them to continue sailing when there was danger of attack. "Some day the pirates may strike your boat by mistake," warned one of the women. "Stay home. We will manage to live somehow until the pirates leave the valley in peace."

Iskander spoke for the cargomen. "The pirates will stay

as long as riches are shipped on the river. Meanwhile, we must earn our living."

The woman shook her head. "How can our men earn their living if they are badly injured?"

Iskander smiled. "You will soon see. I want all the fishermen and the cargo crew to meet in my house after the noon meal. Sayyid Ad-Din, will you come and give us your advice?"

The old scholar had lingered on the bank after leaving the cargo boat. Now he looked at Iskander in surprise. "Eh, I will come. But if you plan to capture the pirates, I must speak against it. That is too dangerous!"

"You'll approve this plan, effendi."

The people began going back to their houses. Iskander glanced over at Yussuf, who had remained alone aboard the freighter. "Come eat with us, Yussuf."

Yussuf smiled and shook his head. "A farmer in the village always sends me food. I must not disappoint him, nor the servant girl who brings the basket. Then I will fasten some cargo that shifted loose as we went around the last bend."

Haroun was disappointed that he wouldn't see Yussuf walking on solid ground. During their boat journey the freighter tilted and pitched in the swift current so that everyone in the boat lurched awkwardly.

As he walked home with Nuri and their parents, Haroun saw coming toward the bank the servant woman who brought meals to Yussuf. She carried a basket and a jug of water and smiled shyly as Iskander's family passed her.

An hour later, when the noon meal was done and Leilah had cleared away the dishes, the fishermen and cargo boatmen gathered in Iskander's house. Haroun and Nuri sat quietly in their sleeping alcove, their curtain raised so they might see all that happened.

Nuri whispered, "Did Father say nothing of his plan as we sailed home?"

Haroun shook his head.

Mahmud trudged in, complaining loudly about losing time for tending his garden. There was also a corner of his roof that needed mending at once. Yussuf hurried in after him. He stumbled, then laughed at his clumsiness and spoke cheerfully to Mahmud.

At last Sayyid Ad-Din entered. The men made way for him, and Iskander set out the best cushion for the scholar. Then, standing before the crowd, Iskander spoke.

"Ever since the pirates came to the River Zeravshan, men have become more and more afraid to sail in the cargo boats that carry valuables between Samarkand and Bukhara. The wages offered men for work in the treasure boats have gone up until, now, the pay has doubled for each journey. My friends, if we could earn this pay, we boatmen would need to work only this summer in order to save all the money we need to buy fishing boats."

Haroun felt a stab of fear. Nuri whispered fiercely, "Rather be poor forever than lose Father to the pirates!"

The men in the room began talking excitedly. Mahmud called out, "Sail in the treasure boats? We would be attacked, maimed for life, perhaps killed!"

Iskander held up his hand for silence. "Not every treasure boat is attacked."

Turbaned heads nodded in agreement. But one of the men said, "That is true, but those carrying the greatest riches are sure to be struck by pirates. And now there are fewer treasure boats sailing, so that it is more likely that the pirates will choose our boat for their attack."

Sayyid Ad-Din rose. "Iskander said to me earlier that he had a plan. Let us hear what it is before we set our hearts against any course of action."

Iskander bowed to the old scholar. "Thank you, effendi. Yes, I have a plan. All up and down the river we are known to carry humble goods, like bales of cotton and bolts of common cloth. Now, if inside these ordinary things there should be concealed gold, silver, jewels, and rare spices, no one would ever guess! We could sail in complete safety."

There was a mutter of amazement. "Eh, perhaps it would work," said Yussuf.

Haroun and Nuri vigorously nodded approval of their father's idea.

Mahmud stood up. "You are foolish to think we would escape the pirates by such a simple trick, Iskander. Do they not have eyes and ears all up and down the river? Somehow, the pirates always know of the rich cargos, though the treasure boats set sail in the night and only friend speaks to friend of happenings on the river."

Mahmud's objection did not bother Iskander. "That is why I asked our fishermen friends to this meeting. They must help us."

"We will gladly help you, Iskander," said one of the fishermen. "What must we do?"

"Go about your fishing as always," said Iskander. "But place your boats here and there along the river, so that during each day of our journey from Bukhara to Samarkand, our freighter is close to Takshan fishing boats. Watch for strangers on the river. With your scimitars and long fish knives aboard, be ready to speed to our aid if we should be attacked by pirates after all."

Sayyid Ad-Din looked at Iskander in wonder. "That is a clever plan indeed, Iskander! If everyone does his part you may carry all the treasure of Bukhara to Samarkand in safety."

Haroun muttered excitedly, "Nuri, we will be fishing with Father once again by autumn!"

"It will never work," growled Mahmud. "The pirates have a spy who will tell them everything."

Sayyid Ad-Din looked alarmed, but Iskander spoke steadily. "No one will know of our plan but the men in this room, and the merchant in Bukhara."

"And who is the merchant in Bukhara?" demanded Mahmud.

"It will be easy to find one," said Iskander. "The traders dealing in valuables are eager to pay any man willing to risk the danger of taking his goods up the Zeravshan. We will leave our own freighter with its owner's partner in Bukhara. Then we will seek out a merchant trading in jewels and precious metals. This cargo we will conceal in bales of wool and cotton in his boat. We will, of course, take our weapons with us as we do now, but I do not think we will have to use them."

The men talked it over as the afternoon grew late.

Iskander described for the fishermen the places along the river where his cargo boat usually moored for the night. The movements of the fishing boats were worked out. At last even Mahmud could find nothing wrong with the plan.

"We need follow this plan only until the autumn rains," said Iskander. "By that time we will have enough money earned to buy our fishing boats."

Sayyid Ad-Din raised his voice. "Do not tell anyone of what we have said in this house today. Do not boast of fooling the pirates. Do not even speak of earning high wages."

Iskander nodded. "You are right, effendi. We must be very careful. It may be true, as some think, that the pirates have a spy."

Haroun thought of the solitary line of crooked footprints leading to a mysterious water gate in Samarkand. And he remembered that both Yussuf and Mahmud had been abroad that dawn. He and Nuri looked at each other.

Perhaps the spy was in that very room.

7

The Secret Messenger

When all the men had left Iskander's house, Haroun and
Nuri showed their father the gold disk. "It's part of the
treasure stolen by the pirates," said Haroun. "We found it
in Samarkand the morning after the Bukhara boat was
attacked." They told Iskander of their adventure beside
the merchant's water gate and how they had later met with
Yussuf. Nuri said, "Mahmud was in the streets, too, walking with a stranger."

Iskander smiled. "And so was Sayyid Ad-Din, coming to
the quay after his night with another scholar. Would you
think him a pirate spy?"

Haroun protested. "Yussuf hid gold on his person."

"So did Mahmud," Nuri insisted.

Iskander examined the gold disk. "Yes, this is one of the many gold ornaments made in Bukhara and carried by the freighter that was attacked. But, Haroun, goldsmiths often send samples of their wares to merchants so that these men can decide what type of goldwork they wish to buy and sell. This gold disk must be one of many types of decoration its maker puts out. The merchant you overheard was doubtless one of the men to whom examples of work had been sent. Then he happened to lose this one."

"The men at the water gate were all acting so mysteriously," Haroun pointed out.

Iskander nodded. "Merchants often do act secretly, especially those dealing with valuables. Eh, these days brothers hardly speak among themselves!" Then Iskander became more serious. "I will not have my sons imagining there are spies among our good men of Takshan."

Haroun dared say, "Yussuf is not of Takshan."

His father looked at him sternly. "He is one of us as long as he chooses to work in the cargo boat." Iskander put away the gold disk and the pieces of jade the boys had found, along with the money Haroun and Nuri had given him from their sale of hawks.

Haroun and Nuri gathered their nets and snares and set out to spend the rest of the afternoon in the hills behind the village. They ran along the main canal, skipping over the ditches leading into the fields and groves. "The water level is sinking," said Nuri. "The banks of the canal are drying."

"The hot season is well upon us," agreed Haroun.

Someone called out to them. It was Zena, gesturing

urgently from her usual seat under the apricot tree. Haroun and Nuri went to her. "Eh, Haroun, I have been watching the hawk. He just flew into the hills. I see him many times. He flies over the river, but today he flew into the hills."

Nuri asked with interest, "What kind of hawk was it?"

The old woman looked puzzled. "I do not know."

Haroun asked gently because it seemed important to her, "Do you remember the colors? That tells us the kind of hawk, and then we know how to set the trap for it."

She stared for a moment, then nodded quickly. "He will fly again and I will watch the colors. Then you can catch him. After that there will be no more pirates."

Haroun was surprised that the old woman had heard of the pirates, since most things were beyond her understanding. In astonishment, Nuri blurted, "What has the hawk to do with pirates?"

Zena smiled cunningly. "He knows. He flies over the river and the hills, and then there comes news of a pirate attack. I sit here and watch the sky, as I promised you I would. I see many hawks, but I see also this same one many times. He always flies before the pirates strike."

Haroun felt sorry for the confused old woman, but Nuri's eyes were widening. "They attack the same day?"

"No," said Zena. "Sometimes the next day, or the day after that. I will watch for the colors, and you will catch him. And then the pirates will attack no more."

Haroun pulled his fascinated brother away. "We have to go now. Good day to you, Zena."

They ran back to the path leading across the fields and

up to the wooded slopes. Nuri was wild with excitement. "The spy is right here in Takshan, Haroun! But what use does he make of a hawk?"

"Pay no attention to that," said Haroun firmly. "Zena had heard bits of news and then put them together in a way that makes sense to her but not to anyone else." He remembered, suddenly, how his father had said much the same about him and Nuri and the gold disk. "Hurry, we have many traps to set before night falls."

In the high wooded hills Haroun and Nuri went to each of their trapping places, recovering the furred or feathered decoys from where they had been hidden in grass and beneath bushes. Carefully they set their snares and nets. As they entered the last clearing, Nuri pointed. "Look, Haroun! That bush is moving, though there is no wind."

Gesturing for silence, Haroun led the way across the field. Within the thrashing bush a small hawk struggled to free itself. It had a slate blue upper body and brown wings. Leather straps round its legs had gotten caught in the branches. "It's a kestrel, like the one you handled," said Haroun. "This one is trained, for it's wearing straps." He threw a net over the hawk and drew on thick gloves. "See, Nuri, it stooped for this decoy. I thought I had it well hidden."

As Haroun carefully freed the kestrel Nuri said, "We must find its owner. Perhaps he's still somewhere in the hills, whistling for his hawk."

"I don't know of anyone in Takshan or the other villages who keeps hawks," said Haroun, calming the kestrel in his hands. "This kestrel must have flown a long way from its master. Hunger made it strike the decoy in the bush."

Nuri pointed to the hawk's leg. "There is something tied here, Haroun."

A tiny roll of parchment was fastened to the hawk's ankle. "Take it off, Nuri." When his brother unrolled the strip, Haroun saw that the parchment was covered with graceful curves and loops.

"This is writing, Nuri. Perhaps it tells the name of the owner and where he lives."

"He may give us a reward when we return the hawk to him! We must find someone who can read it to us," said Nuri eagerly.

"Sayyid Ad-Din can read it," said Haroun. "We'll stop at the mosque on the way home. But first we must finish our work here."

Since they had not brought any falcon socks with them, they emptied the sack of its last net, then carefully wrapped it around the kestrel, leaving only the bird's head and neck free. Then Haroun set the net, baiting it with the same decoy that had lured the kestrel to the bush.

The two started home, going through dim woods and patches of clearing. The late afternoon sun threw long and deceiving shadows across their way. Nuri held the kestrel carefully, watching ahead of him so that nothing could trip him and cause injury to the hawk. They were just skirting a bare low spot in a small field when Nuri exclaimed, "A footprint!" Still holding the kestrel firmly, he bent down to look at it.

Haroun squatted beside him. The low spot had once

been a mudhole, but the heat of summer had turned it into a bed of dried earth. A single footprint at the edge was as hard as the brick used for building houses. There was a wedge-shaped indentation where the ball of the foot would ordinarily be.

Nuri said, "It's the same as the print we saw in Samarkand!"

Haroun nodded. "I wish I could tell if the man who made this print was here before he was in Samarkand, or after."

Nuri said in growing excitement, "Maybe Zena is right! This must be the hawk she always sees, and it really does belong to the pirates. The parchment is a secret message. Haroun, the pirate spy is right here in Takshan!" He stood up, then gasped.

Haroun followed his gaze, then hastily got to his feet.

Only a short distance away Yussuf watched them from the shade of the trees. Haroun wondered how much he had heard them say. As he and Nuri walked toward him, Yussuf waved a casual greeting. "What have you there—a hawk?"

Haroun answered, "Yes, we're taking it home."

"I'll walk with you if you go slowly." Yussuf fell in beside them as they went among the deeply shadowed trees. "I'll carry the kestrel for you, Nuri, so that you may use both hands to keep from stumbling."

Nuri shook his head. "I can carry the hawk easily enough, and I know the way well."

Haroun glanced sharply at Yussuf. In the gloom of the forest he could see only the boatman's usual friendly smile.

Neither of the boys had said what kind of hawk they had. Yet Yussuf knew it was a kestrel. And now Haroun remembered their first trip back from Samarkand. Yussuf had recognized the equipment they had along as hawking gear. But poor men do not keep hawks; and skilled hawkers do not work on cargo boats.

The path started winding down toward the village. It was growing dark very quickly. Once Nuri missed his step and only Yussuf's quick hand saved him from a bad fall. The boatman said, "You should let me carry the kestrel." But Nuri refused to give up the bird.

As they neared the fork where the path branched toward the mosque, Haroun suddenly said, "Yussuf, you are from the city. It must be that you can read."

Yussuf laughed. "City or country, one must study to learn reading. I never went to school, for my family was poor and I had to work." Yussuf gestured toward the ruined minaret rising above the trees. "If you wish to know about reading, you must ask Sayyid Ad-Din, for he is a scholar."

Nuri spoke up. "We are going there now."

Yussuf nodded farewell and continued down the path. Haroun, looking after him, saw the man begin to hurry, and as he did so his right shoulder dipped and rose, dipped and rose. Yussuf was limping!

Nuri spoke impatiently. "Come along, Haroun. It will soon be dark on the paths."

Haroun hurried down the trail of hard-beaten earth. "Yussuf limps," he muttered lest his words carry to the boatman in the clear air. "And what was he doing in the hills? It's lucky we found the kestrel before he did."

Nuri added, "He wanted to take the hawk from me, almost as if he knew about the secret message. What do you think the parchment says?"

"We'll soon find out." Haroun pointed to the mosque garden. "Sayyid Ad-Din is sitting beside his well."

Entering, they went along the stone-paved garden path toward him. The old scholar raised his head at their approach. "Peace to you."

"And to you, peace," replied Haroun. "Effendi, we have found some writing. Will you read it to us?"

Nuri burst out excitedly, "It's a secret message from the river pirates!"

Sayyid Ad-Din sprang up from his seat. "What do you say?" His eyes were wide, his face pale. Suddenly he clutched at his chest and sagged back against the cushions. "Do not play such tricks on an old man. Eh, how you made my heart jump!"

Haroun glared at his brother for startling the scholar. "Effendi, we found the hawk that Nuri holds caught in the brush. This message was tied to its leg." He held out the tiny roll of parchment.

Sayyid Ad-Din looked bewildered. "Hawks? Messages? Here, let me see for myself." He took the strip of parchment from Haroun and held out his hands for the bird. Nuri gave it to him. The scholar held the hawk firmly, pushing the sacking down from its head and shoulders.

Nuri said, "It's a kestrel, effendi."

The scholar looked at the kestrel and then at the rolled parchment strip. He did not open the message. "But why do you speak of pirates?"

Nuri answered. "It was Zena who told us! She noticed

that every time the kestrel flew over Takshan, a pirate raid would come shortly after."

The scholar's hands trembled, then steadied as he stroked the head of the hawk. He smiled in amusement.

"Zena is the old one who sits beneath the apricot tree, is she not? She is beloved of Allah, for no one else can understand what passes through her mind."

Haroun felt embarrassed that the scholar would think they believed everything Zena said. "There is also a footprint, effendi, dried into the mud in the hills. It is the same as the one we saw in Samarkand."

The gray eyebrows rose in surprise and interest. "You must tell me everything, Haroun, for this sounds as if it might be important."

Haroun described how he and Nuri had found the gold disk trampled into the mud beneath the footprint with the peculiar dent. They repeated what they had overheard at the merchant's water gate. Later they had received news of stolen gold. Now the same footprint appeared in the hills, though it may have been made before the one in the soft bank of the Samarkand canal. "There is a connection between the merchant's water gate and Takshan," Haroun insisted. "And now we have found a trained hawk carrying a message. Surely there is a spy among us who tells the pirates of rich cargos." He stopped, hoping the sayyid would uncurl the parchment strip and find that they were right.

The old scholar appeared to be thinking. Then he said, "Have you told this to your father?"

Nuri replied, "Yes, effendi, but he doesn't believe us." He told the sayyid what Iskander had to say of their suspicions only that afternoon, before they went into the hills.

Sayyid Ad-Din, still holding the lost kestrel and its unread message, asked with interest, "Did you go into the woods to gather brush for your mother's cooking fire?"

Haroun explained. "We went much higher than brushgatherers usually do, effendi. In the upper forests we set traps and snares to capture hawks, and then we keep them in the hut behind our garden. This is our new trade. Didn't you see the birds we took to sell in Samarkand?"

The scholar shook his head. "I was meditating during the journey."

Nuri added, "We are saving the money for Father's new fishing boat. When we have enough hawks we'll go to Samarkand again. And perhaps, effendi, we'll go once more to sit beside the merchant's water gate. We may even discover more clues to the pirates!"

The sayyid jerked suddenly. "Eh, this hawk has sharp talons! Was he caught in one of your traps?"

Haroun described how one of their partly hidden decoys had lured the bird into a bush. "And now, effendi, won't you read the message this kestrel carried? Then we'll know if the hawk flies between the pirates and their spy."

Sayyid Ad-Din set the hawk on his lap, and with shaking hands he unrolled the parchment. He studied the curves and loops and then suddenly laughed. "A pirate message, eh? This is nothing but a business note between merchants. A buyer of salt in Bukhara asks his partner in Samarkand if they can send out a caravan in two weeks, for he has the chance to buy a new lot of salt very cheaply."

"Is that all?" cried Nuri.

Haroun, bitterly disappointed, could scarcely believe what he heard. "But, effendi, aren't letters sent by boat and caravan?"

The scholar nodded. "That's true, and they take many days to arrive. A trained hawk, however, is a fast carrier of short messages. These merchants have come upon a clever device to further their trade." He rolled up the parchment strip and once more held the kestrel firmly in his hands. "You did right to bring me the hawk, Haroun. I will send it off once more with its message between the salt merchants."

"There is still the footprint—"

The scholar interrupted impatiently. "Surely your father has judged your story rightly, for he is experienced in the ways of the world. And doesn't one foot sliding into mud look the same as another foot doing the same thing in another place? You must not let your imagination run away." He settled back in his cushions and spoke more kindly. "I am proud that my two young villagers have found a way to earn money for their father. You are clever indeed, and I am interested in how you set your traps. Perhaps you will take me along with you into the hills some day."

Haroun's embarrassment faded under the scholar's interest. "We'll take you gladly, effendi. And later you can come to our house to see how Nuri cares for the hawks until we take them to the merchant."

"It may take many hours to show me all your traps," said Sayyid Ad-Din. "Perhaps your mother will not allow you to be away from home that long."

"We often spend the night in the hills," said Haroun. "Indeed, effendi, we have a great deal of work to do there now that we have returned from Samarkand."

"Then let's set a day for my outing," suggested the sayyid. "Four days hence, late in the afternoon, the same time as it is now. That is when I can take time from my studies."

The boys agreed. "We'll come for you then, effendi."

Sayyid Ad-Din nodded. "Tomorrow, your father leaves on a dangerous venture. Go, and take to him my wishes for success."

Haroun and Nuri left the mosque garden and started along the woods path leading toward the village. Haroun said, "We were wrong about the hawk, Nuri, but I'm certain the footprint is the same as the one in Samarkand!"

8

In Pirate Hands

"Sayyid Ad-Din didn't see the footprints," Haroun continued. "If he had, he wouldn't say the likeness was only an accident. He would see at once that the dent was made by the same broken foot."

"But why would Crooked Foot be in the hills?" Nuri wondered aloud. "We just found out that the hawk doesn't belong to the pirates."

They reached the place where the mosque path joined the other, and they turned down through the dark trees toward the village. Haroun thought over Nuri's question. "If the spy is Yussuf, then he went into the hills to see what we were doing there. But the footprint wasn't made now,

for it is dried. If Yussuf had been up there before, why
would he follow us into the hills again today?"

"He couldn't have been searching for the kestrel," Nuri
said.

Haroun stopped so quickly that Nuri bumped into him.
"The message is between pirates, Nuri, but it's in a code!
Listen, 'salt' might mean 'rubies,' or 'gold,' and the 'next
caravan' could be a boat leaving Bukhara."

Nuri jumped up and down in excitement. "The 'two
weeks' could mean 'two days.' Oh, Haroun, we must warn
them!"

"Warn who, Nuri? We only made this up to see how a
code could be devised to pass on secret messages. Maybe
'salt' really means 'from Samarkand,' and 'caravan' means
'yesterday.' There is no way to understand the message."

"We must go back and tell Sayyid Ad-Din," Nuri insisted.

Haroun shook his head. "He probably has already sent
the kestrel on its way. Besides, he wouldn't believe us. We
can't prove that our idea is true."

They started downward again. The woods path was deep
in shadow. Nuri said, "Haroun, perhaps that message is
about Father's plan to hide valuable cargo in cotton and
wool bales."

"Don't talk foolishly!" Haroun said, suddenly afraid. "If
the spy is Yussuf or Mahmud, as you think, surely he
wouldn't have the pirates attack the very boat in which he
sails!"

Nuri was silent until the trail brought them to the brush-
grown slopes below the woods. Sheep roamed on the hill-

side. Nuri said, "Haroun, the spy can't carry the kestrel with him on the cargo boat, for the others would soon know of it. A hawk must be cared for every day or it will sicken. And if the spy lets it grow too hungry, it will chew through its leash and escape." He hadn't forgotten how his carelessness had caused two of their hawks to work loose in the garden hut.

"I've thought of that," said Haroun. "Everybody knows Father's boat stops at Takshan to visit each week, even staying overnight on the way downstream. The pirates must release their kestrel at that time. The spy then sends the hawk back with whatever news he has gathered. Yussuf wanders alone, as we have seen. He limps, so he must be Crooked Foot."

"Mahmud stays by himself too," Nuri said. "No one ever goes near his house, even while he is gone. The hawk could fly to his apricot orchard and no one would notice."

"But it was Yussuf who came searching for the kestrel," Haroun argued. "He must have seen the hawk above the hills, diving after prey. But the prey was really our lure. We found the hawk in the bush before Yussuf could reach it."

They were in the fields, which were orange with the slanting light of the setting sun. Haroun jumped an irrigation ditch. Nuri, following, said, "Let's pass Mahmud's house. Perhaps we can learn something."

Haroun agreed, and when they reached the village, they turned down the lane leading to Mahmud's home.

Mahmud was digging in the garden next to his orchard. There was a low wall separating it from the lane. Haroun and Nuri slowed as they approached. Nuri nudged Haroun and whispered, "See, there's something gold hanging around his neck."

Mahmud saw them. As he straightened up, a flash of gold disappeared into the folds of his garments. "What are you doing here?"

"We're only going home," Haroun replied. Then he saw freshly piled brushwood. "Were you in the hills today fetching firewood?"

"You will not take any of that wood!" Mahmud ordered sharply. "I spent half the afternoon gathering it in the upper forests. It is to last for my next two visits."

Nuri pointed boldly over the garden wall. "What is that in your garden, Mahmud?"

Among the shadows, Haroun now saw boards staked in the rows of growing plants. Each board was scribbled with curves and loops. "They're signs!" he exclaimed in astonishment. "I didn't know you could read, Mahmud!"

Mahmud pulled his beard in agitation. "No, no, you will not make me say something that is not true. That is not writing."

"I have seen writing," Haroun said. "It looks like that. Why didn't you write the letters to the city mosques when Takshan was seeking a scholar? Instead, Father had to go all the way to Samarkand and hire a scribe."

Mahmud's hands fluttered in dismay. "They are signs that I made to remind me what must be done in the garden, lest I forget between visits." He came toward them and his voice lost some of its sting. "I made up those symbols, for I don't know how to write. See, that circle means this row was thinned on my last visit. That curve with a loop means I set those plants out two visits ago." Mahmud pointed out other signs and explained what they meant. "But if a man who really knew how to read came, he could not tell what these signs meant, for I made them up just for my garden. Plants grow and change, and that makes it hard to remember. The other men have wives and sons to care for their gardens, but I—" He looked down at his empty hands. "I have no one."

Haroun felt touched by an enormous loneliness.

Nuri said suddenly, "I'll care for your garden while you're gone."

Mahmud looked surprised, then angry. "You only want to steal my melons and apricots. Stay away from here. Be off, both of you!"

Haroun and Nuri hastened away, Mahmud's shouts ringing in their ears.

Nuri kicked at a hard lump of earth. "Neither Mahmud nor Yussuf wrote the message carried by the kestrel, because neither man can read."

"Each man says he can't read," Haroun reminded him. "One of them must be lying."

That evening, Haroun and Nuri put the mystery of the pirate spy out of their minds so they could enjoy their father's last hours with them. Early the next day, the boys and their mother said farewell to Iskander on the riverbank. Iskander and the other men swung the cargo boat into the swift current, and soon sailed out of sight beyond the bend.

For three days, Haroun and Nuri worked hard at their

home tasks and their traps in the hills. They caught a big black shaheen and two of the smaller red shaheens. Late in the afternoon of the fourth day they went to the mosque prepared to spend the night in the hills.

Sayyid Ad-Din was waiting for them in the stone-paved garden. "Is the way steep?" he asked anxiously. "Perhaps my old bones cannot make the journey."

"We'll help you, effendi," Haroun promised.

But the scholar climbed better than he thought he would. The three arrived in good time at the trapping area. The first two traps were empty, but Haroun explained to the sayyid how the snares worked and the way the bow nets sprang over the quarry lured by the decoy.

When they started toward another clearing, the scholar excused himself. "You boys go ahead to the other traps. I must return to the mosque, for I am too old to walk for long."

"We will return with you, effendi, and then come back to finish our work," Haroun offered. "There is plenty of time, for Mother said we may spend the night with our traps."

Sayyid Ad-Din shook his head. "I can find the way back myself, and if I grow tired I will rest on the trail." He thanked them for showing him the traps and turned back through the woods.

The shadows were lengthening when Haroun and Nuri came to the next trap. The decoy had been torn to pieces and the snare was sprung. Haroun began making repairs while Nuri handed him what he needed.

Suddenly a shadow sprang before them. Nuri cried, "Haroun—!"

Before Haroun could move, something hard crashed through his turban against his head. He sagged forward into blackness.

Haroun awoke with his head throbbing. Something was holding him fast. He could neither speak nor see. He struggled and found that while his legs were free, his arms were tied behind his back and a sack had been fastened over his head. There was a gag in his mouth.

A rough voice said, "This one is waking up. Quick, bring the horses."

Haroun did not recognize the voice. It could not have been anyone from Takshan, but, hopeful of rescue, he tried to call out in spite of the gag.

He heard the approach of horses, then hands pulled at his knots. "Tight enough," muttered the voice in satisfaction.

No rescuer was this, but captor! The man dragged Haroun over to the horse, then lifted him up behind the saddle. More rope was looped around him, tying him securely to the saddle. Haroun squirmed, trying to find a loose knot, and wondered why these strangers had attacked him.

The man said, "Take that other boy upon your horse."

Another man grunted in exasperation. "This smaller one kicks so! Quiet, you, or I'll knock you unconscious again."

So they had taken Nuri, too! Haroun's heart sank, for now there was little hope that word of the capture would be carried back to Takshan. Even Sayyid Ad-Din was well away toward his mosque. Mother didn't expect them home until the next day.

The man who had tied Haroun to his horse got into the saddle in front of him. "It is well that our friend found these two on his trail. After tonight no one will keep us from plundering every rich cargo boat on the river."

Now Haroun's fear grew, for he and Nuri were in the hands of the pirates. The friend mentioned must mean the man who acted as their spy. Was it Yussuf, who had seen them with the kestrel? Or perhaps it was Mahmud, frightened over their discovery of his writing.

The other man growled, "Be careful how you talk. The boys are bound and gagged, but their ears are not stopped up. Mention no names!"

"It doesn't matter," replied the first man. "These two will never see Takshan again." He laughed, and the horses started up.

Haroun's heart beat very rapidly. What were the men going to do with him and Nuri? Somehow, they must escape. As the horses jogged along, Haroun struggled with his bonds. But he only rubbed his wrists raw against the tight knots.

The journey seemed to last for hours. They jogged up and down, sometimes trotting on a level, and twice galloping for a long way. Then the ground seemed to grow rough once more, with the horses again climbing up and down steep hills. Later there was the sound of running water, growing louder as they neared. Men called out to them, and after a final short gallop, they halted, surrounded by voices.

"Here are the two troublemakers," said the man riding with Haroun.

"They've made trouble for themselves instead," replied a new voice. "You men took long enough getting here."

The first of the riders explained. "We had to avoid all the settlements, and there was a caravan encamped on the open plains. We had to go far around it."

The second rider said impatiently, "We're hungry. Give us food and wine."

"There's meat roasting over the fire. Bring your captives into the cave," ordered the man who seemed to be the pirate chief. "Leave them tied. But be careful not to put them near our weapons."

"They can keep the hawk company," said the first rider. "Come here, you!" Roughly he pulled Haroun from the horse, dragging him along and then pushing him to the ground.

Haroun heard someone else thudding down beside him and guessed that it was his brother Nuri. Though the sack tied over his head kept Haroun from seeing anything, he could hear the crackle of a fire and smell roasting meat. He ached with hunger. Suddenly he heard the fanning of wings and a hawk's gutteral cry.

Haroun listened in astonishment. That was a kestrel's call!

The pirate chief demanded of one of his men, "What, haven't you fed the hawk? You'd better take good care of it, for it's our only way of contacting Gaspar. Without the kestrel, he couldn't send us news of the treasure boats."

Haroun's heart leaped. He and Nuri had been right. The kestrel they had held in their hands only four days ago really did carry pirate messages. After it had flown from

Sayyid Ad-Din's hands, it must have carried another message ordering their capture.

Then Haroun's spirits fell. It was too late for this discovery to do them any good.

The man who seemed responsible for the kestrel answered his chief in a surly tone. "One meal a day is enough for a hawk! If you let that bird have its way, it would gorge itself to death."

Once more the kestrel roused, coaxing for food. It sounded as if it were tethered quite close to Haroun and Nuri.

The hawk keeper exclaimed, "Quiet, you buzzard, or I'll wring your neck!"

"Not yet," warned the pirate chief. "Wait until the end of summer."

"What then?" asked the rider whose horse had carried Haroun. "Do we go back to the desert to rob caravans?"

"Perhaps," answered the chief. "Or we may prey on another river. But first we will spend many months in idle luxury, enjoying the riches brought to us by our daring and our scimitars."

"Eh, the raid tomorrow night may well bring us the richest cargo of all!" said another one of the men. "That Iskander of Takshan is so sure of himself that he plans to sail with an entire cargo of jewels!"

Iskander of Takshan! Then the pirates knew of his father's plan. And they were planning to attack his cargo boat!

Another pirate said, "There will be rare spices hidden in the cotton bales, too."

"Shall we attack the nearest Takshan fishing boats or only slip past them in the night?"

The pirates began discussing the coming raid. Since they knew exactly where the fishing boats would be stationed, they decided to avoid them. The pirates were familiar with the places where Iskander moored each night of his journey, and they planned to attack at the first stop upriver from Takshan. "That way we can retreat toward Samarkand without having to pass Takshan," explained the chief. "The village will be aroused by Gaspar, who must be allowed to escape us without harm."

"Can't he stay out of the freighter?" asked one of the band. "It's harder for us if we have to take care not to hurt him."

"Gaspar must pretend to be one of our victims," said the pirate chief. "Only in this way can he remain entirely free from all suspicion."

Haroun's fear for his father and the men of Takshan turned to anger. Someone in Iskander's boat, known to the pirates as Gaspar, was planning to betray his friends and neighbors. Yet even if they learned Gaspar's identity, Haroun and Nuri were helpless to stop him.

The hawk keeper's voice was complaining. "After you defeat these boatmen, you will take the treasure to Samarkand to hide in the merchant's house, while I stay here in a cave with only the hawk for company!"

"You will keep our captives company as well for a day or so," replied the pirate chief. "In Samarkand I'll arrange with our merchant partner to take these boys away secretly to some distant land, perhaps to the Hind country in the south. There they can be sold as slaves. Even if they manage to escape their new masters, it will be impossible for them to cross the great mountains to find their way home. They'll never see the River Zeravshan again."

As the pirates' laughter echoed through the cave, Haroun jerked his wrists fiercely against the tight ropes.

The pirate chief spoke again. "Let's get some sleep. You, stand guard outside the cave. And you, fetch a jar of water to put out the fire. You, see that the boys are still securely bound."

Haroun heard the soft shuffle of slippers on the hard floor of the cave. Hands tugged at his bonds as they had in the hills above Takshan. "Hungry, are you?" taunted a voice above him. "You'll miss many more meals before you eat slave food."

The pirates moved to another part of the cave, and soon everything was quiet but for the rushing waters of the river.

Exhausted by hunger and fear, Haroun fought off sleep. He had only the few hours from now until dawn to flee certain slavery and to warn his father of the impending attack. Desperately he worked against his bonds. Then his fingers encountered Nuri's. Both boys struggled to sit up, back to back, and tried to untie each other. But all their efforts were useless.

Haroun struggled over to the wall of the cave. Patiently he began sawing his ropes against the rock. But the stone crumbled away easily without cutting.

The hawk, alarmed by Haroun's movements, roused with a fanning of wings.

And then Haroun knew how they would escape from the cave.

9

Escape to Danger

Haroun lay still long enough to be certain the pirates were sleeping soundly. The guard outside the cave would have his ears filled with the rushing current of the river. Haroun could move about with no fear of discovery.

Slowly he worked his way over the cave floor toward where he had heard the men talking as they sat around the fire. His exploring fingers found wet ashes and damp charred wood. Then he came across greasy scraps of roasted meat.

Straining to reach the ropes that fastened his wrists together, Haroun rubbed his bonds thoroughly with the meat scraps. Carefully he moved back to Nuri next to the cave wall. From the hawk's earlier sounds, he knew the kestrel must be tethered somewhere quite close.

Working his shoulders against the wall of the cave, Haroun struggled to his feet. A flutter of wings guided him. There was an eager squawk and then Haroun stumbled up against a large wooden peg driven waist high into the cave wall. Here the kestrel was perched. Haroun turned his back to the hawk, holding out his roped wrists with their smell of meat. He felt a sharp stab at his bonds, and soon the kestrel was picking away hungrily at the rope. The first strand snapped under the sharp beak, then another. The hawk paused, seemingly puzzled.

Haroun lowered himself to the cave floor and once more labored over to the fireplace to rub more meat scraps on the rope. Once again the hawk tore at his bonds. Haroun helped by pulling his wrists apart. Finally the last of the shredded strands broke free.

Haroun rubbed his sore wrists, then, finding the knots that held the sack over his head, he untied them and removed the sack, knocking his turban loose. He untied the rags that gagged him and then rested a moment, blinking in the darkness.

Feeling for Nuri, Haroun soon untied him. When Nuri could speak, he whispered, "We must hurry and warn Father!"

Haroun murmured, "There's a guard outside. Stay behind me."

The kestrel squawked, perhaps seeking the food that smell and taste had promised. When the pirates discovered Haroun and Nuri's escape in the morning, they might send a message changing their plans. But if they had to keep to the plan they had already made with their spy, then Iskander would know how to meet the threat to his cargo boat. Haroun picked up one of the sacks that had covered their heads. Feeling for the kestrel's perch, he found the tether frayed from the hungry bird's pecking. It was easy to snap the worn leash. He placed the hawk in the sack, knotting the long loose end. The kestrel became as quiet as if in a falcon sock. Then Haroun began feeling his way along the rock wall toward the cave entrance. Nuri followed closely.

Rounding a bend, Haroun saw faint light ahead, as of starlight reflected from the river. The roaring of the current grew louder as the boys approached the opening.

A sudden gleam caught Haroun's eye. Two or three scimitars lay carelessly just inside the cave. Stooping, he picked up two, giving one to Nuri. They thrust them through their waistbands.

Peering through the starlit trees and bushes outside the cave, Haroun saw the turbaned head of the guard and the gleam of his weapons some distance away at the edge of the water. The pirate was standing, not on the bank of the great River Zeravshan as Haroun had thought, but alongside a swift stream that went charging down a steep defile. It probably swept into the larger river, for in the distance and over the rush of the stream Haroun could hear the deeper boom of the Zeravshan current.

The guard was gazing steadily downstream, his back to the cave. Haroun nudged Nuri, then led the way out of the cave. Stooping, they crept into the brush of the overgrown

bank. A little way upstream, a clump of trees shadowed the stream. Haroun guided Nuri there, and they waded across in cold water that surged up to their chests. Haroun held the kestrel in its sack high above the swift current.

On the other bank they paused to wring out their garments, and then began working their way downstream. The stream reflected just enough starlight for them to see their path. They drew abreast the pirate guard. Near him massed shadows much thicker than trees or boulders. Haroun suddenly understood. "Nuri, he's not guarding the cave. Those must be the pirate boats pulled up on the bank, and they are what he watches."

"I wish we could push them into the stream so they'd get wrecked," Nuri muttered.

But Haroun soon saw that they would be lucky just to avoid the alert guard. He put his mouth to Nuri's ear. "We must creep slowly, as if coming upon a hawk alight, with our nets ready."

On hands and knees they slowly and sometimes painfully worked their way among the bushes and stones beside the stream. Once Haroun paused to tie the long end of the hawk sack to his waistband, thus freeing both hands. They had hardly started again when Nuri accidentally kicked a stone. It rattled over pebbles and splashed into the stream, a loud clatter above the wash of current. Both of them stopped as they watched the guard staring in their direction. It was a long time before they could resume their slow progress along the overgrown bank. Then Haroun found they were moving toward the right and he realized the stream was rounding a bend.

On the other side of the bend, hidden by cliffs, he and Nuri stood up. Haroun grinned in the darkness. "Now we can make our way quickly to the River Zeravshan."

"But how are we to reach Father's boat?" asked Nuri, "By now it must be a day's sail below Takshan, and I don't know where we are."

Haroun didn't want to think about that problem now. "We'll find a way somehow."

They traveled more quickly along the stream, and found that it emptied into a larger, more slowly moving one. This too they followed downstream, toward the louder roaring of the Zeravshan. Finally they stood on the reed-grown banks of the great river itself. All the land about was a wilderness of scrub growth.

Nuri spoke above the current's rumbling. "Which way to Takshan? If only we could meet some friendly villagers!"

"We can, Nuri! Remember Father's plan? The fishermen agreed to station themselves up and down the river to watch for any trace of pirates. We have only to go along the bank until we find a Takshan fishing boat. The men will take us to Father!" He began walking downstream, following the River Zeravshan toward distant Bukhara. Nuri scrambled after him.

The way along the bank was very rough and overgrown. Sometimes tall reeds massed so thickly that they had to climb through them as if through a forest. After a long time the ground leveled and smoothed, and soon they found a regularly used path. Then they passed a huddle of neatly kept houses. "A village," said Haroun. "I wish I knew which it was." He envied the people sleeping peacefully in their own homes.

A long time later, after passing orchards and cultivated fields, they came to another village. Not far beyond it Haroun made out the looming hulk of a fishing boat moored to trees growing along the shore. As they went toward it, Nuri said worriedly, "Suppose it's not a Takshan boat?"

"It's moored in the river, not pulled up on the bank like the boats whose men are home for the night." He squinted at the dark craft in the starlight. The lines were familiar and even without seeing the owner's mark painted on the prow, Haroun knew the boat was from Takshan. He called out and instantly a turbaned head appeared. "Who calls in the night?"

"Haroun, son of Iskander, and Nuri, his brother. You know us."

"Haroun and Nuri! What has happened? Come aboard. I'll waken my uncle at once."

Soon the boys were huddled around a fire in a brass brazier, eating hot rice with pieces of fish in it. They told the two fishermen they had been captured in the hills and taken to the pirate cave where they overheard plans to rob Iskander's freighter at the first mooring place upriver from Takshan. "We managed to escape while they slept, and now we must hurry to warn Father," said Haroun urgently. There was much more to tell—the gold disk, the footprints. . . . Haroun's head buzzed with weariness. Nuri's eyes were closing. The spy . . . and the hawk. . . .

The older fisherman smiled. "Sleep then, Haroun. You

have told us the important part. We will take you to
Iskander as quickly as possible. The wind is right—we can
meet his freighter by dawn."

Up went the sail. The mooring lines snaked aboard. A
turn of the tiller sent the fishing craft into the swift Zeravshan current.

Nuri slumbered against the railing. Haroun fed the
kestrel bits of fish, then placed the bird back in the sack.
Curling up, he went to sleep.

Haroun was shaken out of his sleep by a big hand on his
shoulder. He blinked in the pale dawn. Beside him Nuri
was yawning. The younger fisherman said, "We have met
your father's boat and told him of your adventure. He
wants you to come aboard."

Tied to the bank was a cargo boat, its deck piled high
with bales of cotton and bolts of common cloth. The
freighter was like the craft sailed by the Takshan men for
the Samarkand textile merchant. Only this cargo, Haroun
knew, contained hidden treasure. The crewmen were
holding the fishing boat by its mooring lines. Iskander
stood beside the mast. Nuri quickly climbed aboard the
freighter. Haroun gathered up their scimitars and the
hawk in its sack and followed.

Iskander embraced his two sons. "Allah be praised; you
are safe now!" The crewmen tossed off the fishing craft's
lines. Iskander waved a farewell, calling out, "Carry the
word, as we agreed!"

"Yes, all will go well," replied the fishermen. The boat
began working up against the current.

Iskander led the boys to where Yussuf was preparing

breakfast in a brazier. "Eat, and then tell me of your capture and escape. The fishermen told us what they knew, but many questions remain."

Haroun was uneasy as he ate. He could see Nuri fidgeting uncomfortably. The crewmen finished their morning meal quickly and went about their work. Haroun muttered to his younger brother, "How can we speak to Father with Yussuf about?"

Nuri murmured in answer, "It's Mahmud's ears I fear!"

When Iskander came to sit beside the boys, Haroun said at once in a low voice, "Father, the pirates said their spy would be aboard your boat."

Iskander raised his eyebrows in surprise. "But no one is here except the usual boatmen!"

Nuri added, "I, too, heard what the pirates said." Suddenly he jumped up and leaped about the deck. "Ow! My leg has a cramp! Ow, ow! Let me run along the bank, Father!" He jumped over the railing and ran up and down the bank. Iskander and Haroun followed him off the boat. Nuri led them far down the bank and then stopped.

Iskander said, "You didn't fool me with your cramp, Nuri. I know you wanted to get us away from the rest of the crew."

Haroun grinned and Nuri looked rueful. "But my leg does hurt," he insisted, rubbing the muscle of his calf. "And the spy is aboard your boat. We heard the pirates say so while they held us prisoner."

Iskander stroked his beard in thought. "But how could two boys become such a threat to the pirates that they had to be taken captives?"

"It was because of the hawk," Haroun said. He explained how they had found the trained kestrel with a message on its leg. Though the note Sayyid Ad-Din had read seemed innocent, it could still have been a code between the pirates and their spy. "The men who carried us to the cave on their horses said that the spy found us on his trail and became afraid of discovery. Yussuf knew we had caught a trained kestrel, and he saw us discover an old footprint he had made in the hills. He made the same footprint in the mud beside the water gate in Samarkand!"

Iskander began to protest, but Nuri added quickly, "The spy must be a Takshan man, Father! The pirates call him Gaspar and they said he would be in the boat. Gaspar will be allowed to escape so he can rouse Takshan and play the part of an innocent victim of the attack. I think Mahmud is Gaspar. He became frightened when we discovered he could read and write secret messages. When Sayyid Ad-Din released the kestrel we gave him, the hawk must have flown right to Mahmud. He wrote a new message, ordering our capture, and then went off to Bukhara in your boat."

Iskander held up his hand. "I am forced to agree that the spy seems to know Takshan and our crewmen very well. Tell me everything you can remember, but do not name either Yussuf or Mahmud. I shall decide if any of our men must be accused. Haroun, how many pirates are there, and when exactly do they plan to attack our boat?"

Together, Haroun and Nuri told of their adventure in detail. Iskander nodded gravely over their words, and when they were finished he looked troubled. "It doesn't seem possible that one of the crewmen can be a pirate spy, for all of them have worked hard and willingly. Yes, even Mahmud, though he mutters and complains. We can only wait and watch and hope that this Gaspar will betray himself, if indeed he is in my boat. I prefer to think that the spy is still in Takshan."

Haroun exclaimed, "The hawk will know Gaspar, Father! We have only to release the bird and it will fly straight to the hand it knows."

Iskander added, "Or it will fly back to the pirate cave, or lose itself in the forested hills above Takshan. If that happens we still haven't proved who spies for the pirates. No, Haroun, keep the kestrel. Perhaps later we will find a way for the hawk to expose Gaspar."

Nuri said, "But what of the attack that's planned?"

Iskander smiled. "It's being turned into a trap for the pirates. Already word is being carried among the Takshan fishing boats. Meanwhile, we will pretend that we know nothing of the pirate plans."

"If Gaspar is among the crew as we think," muttered Haroun, "the pirates may soon learn that you've been warned."

His father laid a hand on his shoulder. "Guard the hawk well so no word can be sent to the pirates. If someone should free the kestrel, he could claim it was by accident, and again, nothing is proven. Perhaps I should keep the hawk with me when I leave you off at Takshan."

"Put us off the boat? No, Father, please!" exclaimed Haroun. Someone aboard had to see whether Yussuf tried to signal the pirates.

"We want to face the pirates with you," protested Nuri.

It was Haroun who thought of the best reason for staying aboard. "With our escape from the cave, the pirates may be watching the river closely. If you don't want them to know you've been warned, Nuri and I must not be seen aboard. We should stay hidden in the cargo."

Nuri added, "Mother won't be worried, for we planned to stay in the hills today."

"She will worry if you are not home by nightfall." Iskander tugged at his beard thoughtfully. "It's true that, if the spy is around Takshan, as I think, your return might make the pirates change their plans. The raid is to come close enough to the village so that Gaspar could warn the pirates not to attack. Our boat would escape, but the river would still be plagued by these brigands." He sighed deeply. "I wish I could avoid it, but it seems that I must keep you with me. Alas, Haroun and Nuri, you have escaped from peril only to face more danger!"

10

Iskander Sets a Trap

"When the pirates attack us tonight," Iskander went on, "we'll be moored in a bend a good distance above Takshan. You boys must remain hidden in the cargo all day. It'll be hot and uncomfortable."

"We won't mind," Haroun and Nuri said together.

Iskander continued. "We cargomen with our scimitars will bait a trap for the pirates according to plans we made before breakfast. Word is already being carried to the Takshan fishing boats along the river, explaining their part in tonight's surprise. Now let's return to our craft. We must continue our journey as if we did not suspect any danger."

Haroun asked, "When the pirates approach our

freighter tonight, won't their spy shout a warning to them?"

"The spy must be in Takshan," Iskander said. "I spoke only in Takshan about my plans to conceal the rich cargo. And I know my crewmen well, Haroun. There is no traitor among them."

As the three walked along the bank toward the waiting cargo boat, Haroun muttered to Nuri, "It is for us to watch for the spy among the crew."

His younger brother nodded. "I'll look out for Mahmud, and you can watch—Haroun! Yussuf is at our hawk sack!"

The boys ran ahead along the bank and leaped aboard the freighter. Yussuf was bending over the sack they had left in the bow. He straightened as they came. Nuri took the sack in his arms.

Yussuf said, "Is that the hawk you had when the pirates captured you? If so, you must let it have water, for this is the hot season when the earth dries and creatures thirst."

Before either of the boys could reply, the kestrel itself squawked pleadingly from within the folds of the sack. Haroun said, "We'll see that it has water."

When Yussuf went to the stern of the boat, Nuri asked, "Do you think he knows this is the same kestrel we carried to Sayyid Ad-Din?"

"Perhaps that was what he wanted to see."

Iskander came aboard and gave the order to set the great square sail and cast off the mooring lines. While the crew used long poles to help the freighter work against the current, Haroun and Nuri made a hiding place among the bales of cotton and bolts of cheap cloth.

It was hot and dark inside, not pleasant like the snug niche they had made returning from their second visit to Samarkand. "I wish there were room to spread the bales farther apart," said Haroun. "Now wait here while I get our scimitars and the hawk."

Haroun pushed aside the cloth hanging before the entrance to their hiding place. The river breeze was wonderfully cool after the stuffiness inside. He found their scimitars in the bow, but his heart jumped when he saw that the hawk sack was missing. Had Yussuf dared to take it after all?

Instantly Haroun scanned the broad skies above the great river, but no bird wheeled overhead, searching for prey. He glanced around the cargo boat. Yussuf was coiling rope. Two other men were poling, while a third was patching the spare sail.

Mahmud, hunched over, was busy with something at his feet.

Haroun ran, dodging mounds of cargo, and came to Mahmud just as the man had uncovered the head and shoulders of the kestrel. Opening its sharp beak, the bird squawked a protest.

Haroun shouted, "Here, give me my hawk!"

Startled, Mahmud let the sack drop from his hands. The kestrel wriggled loose from the folds of cloth. Haroun lunged, and gathered the cloth once more around the hawk. He faced Mahmud. "You—you thief!"

The old man shook his fist. "Thief, am I, to relieve suffering? Letting a bird lie in the hot sun—that is the sort of cruelty a thoughtless boy like you would commit!"

Haroun returned to the hiding place, both angry at Mahmud and ashamed of his own carelessness. Someone had given Nuri a large jar of water, and Haroun cupped a handful to let the kestrel drink. He then sprinkled the hawk's body.

He and Nuri remained concealed all day, their hands but a touch away from the real cargo of jewels and spices concealed within the common goods. They devised various word and guessing games to pass the time. Still the hours dragged along in heat and boredom.

They had just finished the midday rice that Yussuf had brought them when they felt the boat shuddering to a stop. "What's happening?" asked Nuri in the gloom of their cotton-bale cave. "Have we struck a sandbar?"

"Father said we'd reach Takshan around noon," answered Haroun. "He plans to stop only long enough to walk home with Mother and tell her where we are."

The freighter jerked sharply as the crew forced it out of the current and alongside the bank. The boys heard the shouts of greeting. The talk soon faded, and no one was left aboard but Yussuf. The boat's short stop seemed very long. Nuri fell asleep, but Haroun suffered in the still hot air of their prison and longed for a melon from the home garden.

Finally Haroun heard the growing murmur of people gathering at the bank. Men clambered aboard, and ropes thumped to the deck. Suddenly there were urgent shouts from the bank. Iskander called back, but Haroun could not make out his words. There was more shouting, then a series of creaks and bumps that Haroun could not place.

After a muffled argument on the deck, there were the familiar sounds and movements of the freighter once more getting under way and the farewell shouts of the villagers.

Nuri woke up. "Are we moving?"

Haroun peered out from their curtained quarters. "Nuri, someone has come aboard. It—it is Sayyid Ad-Din!"

Nuri was beside him at once. "Why did Father take him aboard, Haroun? Won't he be in danger when the pirates strike tonight?"

The questions went unanswered through the long hot afternoon as they crouched in hiding. The cargo boat went upstream, sometimes fighting against the swift current, and other times gliding smoothly through the slackwater at the side of a broader section of the river.

At last there were the shudders and bumps that meant they had arrived at the usual mooring place, a large bend nearly shut off by sandbars. Peering from behind the curtain, Haroun watched the crew work the boat through the narrow entrance to the calm water of the inlet. They moored the freighter in the shadows of the trees that grew thickly along the sandy bank.

Haroun and Nuri could hear the idle talk of the boatmen as they made the evening meal. Through the little space between curtain and cotton bales they could see Sayyid Ad-Din strolling up and down the deck.

It was dark by the time Iskander came to their hiding place. He thrust aside the curtain; Haroun could just make out Sayyid Ad-Din beside Iskander in the starlight. The moon had not yet risen. Iskander handed in their supper bowls. "My sons," he said, speaking softly. "I have just told our good sayyid how you came to be aboard my boat and the reason you must stay hidden. I could not speak of this before the villagers of Takshan, and refusing to take the sayyid aboard would have looked suspicious."

"Had I known this," said the old scholar, "I would not have insisted on my trip to Samarkand. Pirates! To capture these poor boys! And they plan to attack the boat tonight, you say?" His shadowy form drew up indignantly. "No, Iskander, I cannot hide from danger. I will stand before these brigands and demand their surrender."

Iskander shook his turbaned head. "They won't believe you are a scholar, effendi, for they are accustomed to treachery. You'll be harmed in the fighting." He spoke to Haroun. "Set yourself before the entrance and keep your scimitar ready. In case the hiding place is discovered during the raid you must protect the sayyid at all cost! Now, effendi, I beg you to go in."

The boys moved aside to make room for the old scholar. Haroun carefully placed the hawk, still in its sack, in a far corner. With mutterings and sighs the sayyid crowded into the cotton-bale cave. Haroun and Nuri handed back their empty supper bowls and Iskander dropped the curtain in place.

Sayyid Ad-Din spoke in the darkness. "I have business at the mosques in Samarkand. And now I understand why your father was unwilling to take me aboard this noon. Ah, had he but warned me of pirates—"

Haroun said, "He could not do that without alerting the pirate spy he believes is in Takshan, effendi. And Father's whole plan depends on surprise."

Nuri added, "But we think the spy is aboard this boat, effendi. Haroun and I will be watching for him to reveal himself when the pirates attack."

Sayyid Ad-Din said, "This bloodshed can be stopped. Haroun, Nuri, you must help me! When the pirates approach I must cry out to demand their surrender."

Nuri protested, "But, effendi—"

Haroun said quickly, "The attack will come at moonrise, two hours away. Let's get what sleep we can until then." He nudged his brother with a slippered foot.

Nuri hastily agreed, and they settled themselves in their cramped quarters with heads near the curtained entrance. Haroun raised the cloth a little, both to catch the river breeze and to watch the dark night, silent except for the constant roar of the current.

The three lay still. Haroun wondered if the old scholar were asleep. With luck, the sayyid would not awaken until the pirates actually clashed with the Takshan men. Then the well-meaning scholar would not spoil Iskander's surprise. And to make certain the spy did not, there was the scimitar at Haroun's side.

Time passed slowly in the warm night. Haroun and Nuri could not keep from shifting their cramped positions. Occasionally Sayyid Ad-Din stirred and muttered, but he still seemed asleep. The hawk, well-fed and watered, lay quietly in its sack in the corner.

When the moon rose Haroun could make out the still forms of the crew lying on deck as if sleeping. He found the familiar outline of Yussuf in his ragged chapan. Nuri whispered, "I see Mahmud. He is next to Yussuf." Then Nuri caught his breath. "Haroun, the pirates!"

Shadows moved at the mouth of the inlet. Above the river's roaring sounded the sharper splashes of long poles. Three fishing boats began closing with the moored freighter.

Haroun stared at one of the boats. The sweep of the railing, the angle of the prow, and all the other lines were as familiar to him as his home in Takshan. "Nuri—that is Father's boat!"

Suddenly Sayyid Ad-Din's head moved. The scholar raised himself, wide awake, and reached for the curtain.

Haroun whispered, "No, effendi! You will spoil the trap!"

But Sayyid Ad-Din began to struggle past Haroun and Nuri. "Out of my way!" he hissed. "I must do my duty."

"You'll be in danger!" Haroun warned. "They'll harm you!"

The scholar pushed past him heedlessly. Desperately, Haroun swung his scimitar. The heavy bronze hilt struck the old man's head and he sank back with a groan, turban awry.

Nuri exclaimed in a low voice, "Haroun! What have you done?"

"It was the only way to save him from harm." Haroun put an ear close to the sayyid. "He breathes easily, Nuri." He sighed with relief.

Nuri peered beyond the curtain. "The attack is coming. Mahmud has not yet moved. Nor Yussuf."

Grappling irons thudded on the railing of the cargo

boat. From the three fishing boats the pirates clambered aboard. There were seven of them, one for each of the Takshan men, for the spy would have to at least pretend to fight. And the pirates were hardened and vicious battlers.

Haroun recognized the voice of the pirate chief. "They're asleep. The boys haven't been able to warn them after all. Put up your weapons, and throw these men into the river! But awaken Gaspar first, that he may safely get away."

The pirates went to the figures lying here and there on deck. Haroun held his breath. Which one would Gaspar be? Suddenly all the seemingly sleeping men jumped up, scimitars flashing in the moonlight. The pirates cried out in surprise, fumbling for their own weapons, but not before at least one of them was badly wounded.

Above the rumbling of the River Zeravshan came the rasping of blade against blade. As shadows struggled in the moonlight, Haroun lost sight of both Yussuf and Mahmud. Shouts of warning and cries of pain scored the night. Feet thumped along the deck.

Haroun, peering from beneath the curtain of the hideout, could make out little more than the flash of weapons and the tangle of shadowed limbs. Nuri whispered anxiously, "Who's winning?"

"Our men are just holding their own."

Suddenly Iskander uttered three piercing cries.

Haroun said, "The signal! Soon now they'll—"

"See, already they're coming!" said Nuri. "But why doesn't the spy warn the pirates?"

More shadows massed along the sandbars of the inlet.

One by one they slipped through the narrow entrance. In the cargo boat the noise and confusion of fighting kept the pirates from noticing the approach of the five Takshan fishing craft. And still the spy did not cry a warning.

Poling swiftly through the shallow water, the fishermen quickly reached the freighter and swarmed aboard, scimitars swinging.

"Treachery!" cried the pirate chief, swiftly cornered by two men near the foot of the mast. Slashing furiously with his scimitar, he drove away his attackers. But more Takshan men rushed toward him.

Sayyid Ad-Din groaned and sat up. "Oh, my head! That noise—it sounds like fighting. What is happening?"

"The trap has sprung!" said Nuri gleefully.

Haroun saw the pirate chief jump up on the bow railing. The brigand was shouting something to his followers. Haroun cried, "The pirates are being driven off, Nuri!" He stood up, pulling off the cloth that covered the hiding place. Nuri jumped up on a cotton bale next to him. Sayyid Ad-Din, still confused, slowly straightened up beside them.

Haroun saw the pirates break away one by one from their attackers. They ran to where their chief stood on the bow railing with his deadly scimitar sweeping a space clear. The pirates leaped into the shallow water and struggled to the bank and were soon lost in the heavy growth of trees. Their chief was the last to leave the cargo boat. He had not yet reached the riverbank when the Takshan men jumped overboard after the brigands.

Nuri ran to the railing. Haroun, snatching up the

kestrel for safekeeping, followed his brother. They were both just climbing overboard when Sayyid Ad-Din suddenly crowded past them. Dropping into the water, the sayyid made his way toward the bank with surprising speed, reaching it at the same time as the pursuing Takshan men.

Haroun and Nuri followed as quickly as they could. When they reached the wet sand of the bank they heard milling confusion within the trees. They went through the growth to find the Takshan men on a damp sandy path running beside the river. Yussuf came limping along the trail. "Hurry, I tell you I saw them going upstream!"

Sayyid Ad-Din's voice held scorn. "You saw trees moving in the breeze. The pirates ran this way, and I saw them myself."

"Bah!" said Mahmud sourly. "They have surely fled farther away from the river to hide in deep brush."

Iskander said, "We must hasten after them, or they will escape. Split into three groups!"

"That is not wise," said the scholar. "Come this way at once."

The kestrel in its sack wriggled under Haroun's fingers. "Father, now let's see who our spy is!" He tore open the sack.

"Haroun, not here!" cried Iskander.

But he was too late. The hawk was in Haroun's hands, then suddenly it sprang free. With a loud squawk it fluttered straight toward the man it knew.

Iskander cried, "Sayyid Ad-Din! This is surely a mistake!"

The old scholar waved his arms at the fluttering hawk. "Begone! Take it away!" He staggered backwards on the sandy path.

"It's no mistake!" shouted Haroun. "Sayyid Ad-Din is the pirate spy!"

11

Through the Gate

Haroun pointed to a patch of wet sand at the old scholar's feet. Showing plainly in the moonlight were the wedgelike imprints of a once-broken foot. "See, it is Sayyid Ad-Din who made the crooked footprint we saw in Samarkand and again in the hills above Takshan."

The old man stared at the footprints, then looked fearfully at the men around him. With a cry of desperation he whirled and darted away.

Mahmud shouted, "Spy, are you?" He was after the man in an instant, pulling him to the ground by his long rich robes.

Yussuf spoke up. "So it was not trees in the wind that I saw, but the pirate band slipping away."

Iskander swiftly ordered, "Mahmud, you and my sons stay here to guard Sayyid Ad-Din. Yussuf and I and the others will follow the pirates. Let's take care not to enter any trap they may have waiting for us along the trail." With his scimitar poised, Iskander led the men into the shadows along the upstream path.

Mahmud stood over Sayyid Ad-Din, his scimitar in his hand. "Haroun, fetch rope to tie up this scoundrel. Nuri, take care of the hawk."

Sayyid Ad-Din snarled, "If it had not been for that hawk—" Then he fell silent.

When Haroun returned with a rope from the cargo boat, Mahmud quickly tied the old scholar's hands and feet. Nuri found the kestrel perched in a tree and placed it once more in the sack from which Haroun had released it.

Haroun saw a dark stain on the sleeve of Mahmud's tunic. "Mahmud, you were wounded in the fighting!"

The older man shrugged. "It's but a scratch. Eh, I was glad to do my part with the other men of Takshan."

This was the first time Haroun had known Mahmud to miss an opportunity to complain, and it surprised him.

Then in the distance they heard the rasping sounds of steel against steel. Nuri jumped up. "They've found the pirates!"

Haroun picked up his scimitar. "That sounds like fighting!"

He bounded toward the upstream path, but Mahmud stopped him. "Your father said you are to stay here and guard our prisoner."

Reluctantly Haroun went back to sit on a tree root. It

was hard to stay behind and listen to the distant sounds of the clash. Worse to bear was the long sudden silence that followed. And then there was the welcome sound of friends coming up the path. All the Takshan men gathered in the clearing with the seven pirates as captives.

"We need rope," said Iskander. "Yussuf, tie up these brigands. Haroun, you were among the pirates for some hours. Can you tell if all the pirates are here or if some have stayed behind in their cave?"

"There were seven," said Haroun, for he had carefully counted the different voices he had heard around the fire. "One was to stay behind to guard us, but after we escaped they must have decided to let him come along."

Nuri pointed to Sayyid Ad-Din who had been bound and was sitting on the sand. "And that's the one they call Gaspar."

The pirate chief twisted around to look. "Gaspar! How did—?"

Sayyid Ad-Din said, "They made the kestrel point to me as the spy. I always said it was risky using a hawk to carry messages."

Mahmud shook his head in wonder. "How is it that you, a scholar, a learned man, came to work with pirates?"

Yussuf reached down and pulled off Sayyid Ad-Din's turban. "See, his beard is gray, but his hair is black and thick. He only pretended to be old. Perhaps he is not even a scholar."

Mahmud nodded. "He was strong enough when I stopped him from running away."

The man at his feet admitted, "It's true. I'm not a

scholar. Gaspar is my real name, and I'm one of the pirate band."

The pirate chief shouted, "Silence! Tell them nothing!"

Gaspar raised his head. "There's no harm saying that the real Sayyid Ad-Din died on the caravan journey from Merv."

Haroun exclaimed, "Sayyid Byram in Samarkand heard that news and repeated it to us, but we told him he was mistaken!"

Iskander demanded, "Did you cause harm to the real Sayyid Ad-Din?"

The pirate chief said, "No, no! Even we would not harm a holy man. Sayyid Ad-Din died of old age."

Iskander asked more questions, but the pirates stubbornly refused to answer.

Yussuf said, "They think silence will lessen their guilt."

"They will speak to the Governor of Samarkand's guards," said Iskander. "Let's start upriver with them at once."

The men of Takshan carried the bound pirates aboard the cargo boat. The three stolen fishing craft would be towed back to Takshan by the fishermen. Only the smaller boat of Mahmud was missing. Gaspar said it had smashed into a cargo boat during a raid and had sunk.

As they untied the mooring lines, Haroun heard Mahmud grumbling to the other crewmen. "Bah, it is well for you that you can go back to fishing. As for me, I will surely drag up and down this river for the rest of my days."

Yussuf paused to put a hand on the older man's shoulder. "Allah takes away, old one, but remember that Allah also gives. Eh, before long perhaps you will have a son."

Mahmud looked at him wonderingly. "You have been a good friend to me, Yussuf. But even you can't make such a promise."

The freighter moved upriver all night long, the men taking turns for short periods of rest. None of the boatmen slept, fearing the pirates would manage to escape. Haroun and Nuri tried to keep awake, but sleep finally claimed them.

When they awoke late the next morning, the boatmen were weary and gaunt-eyed from lack of sleep. That afternoon they entered Samarkand and threaded through the maze of canals to arrive before the domed and towered palace of the Governor.

The guards asked them their business. When Iskander explained that they had captured the river pirates, the guards took charge of the prisoners and led the Takshan men to a room where they told their story to the Captain of Guards. Then they were given water, for washing, and fresh garments. Food was set out for them.

They had hardly finished eating when the Captain of Guards returned. "The pirates refuse to speak of their deeds. Do you men know of any proof that will make them confess their crimes?"

Haroun exclaimed, "The merchant of the water gate! He sells their stolen goods for them."

The Captain asked quickly, "Where does he live?"

Nuri jumped to his feet. "Here in Samarkand, effendi! We can show you the way."

"We even know the secret signal," Haroun said.

Late that night, when the moon was beginning to sink in the sky, two boats moved silently along the dark, deserted canals of Samarkand.

Haroun and Nuri leaned over the bow of the leading boat. Behind them, crouching out of sight, were a dozen of the Governor's armed soldiers. Beside them stood the Captain of Guards, bending his helmeted head to Haroun's directions, and relaying them in whispers to the man who stood at the tiller.

Haroun muttered, "Under this bridge, then just before the next bend on the left side. . . ."

Poles dipped silently. Then at last, under muttered orders, they dug deeply into the canal silt, holding the boat and halting the one that followed.

The Captain spoke to Haroun and Nuri. "We must wait until the moon drops behind the Great Minaret. By then other soldiers will be guarding the archway so no one can escape through the streets."

Anxiously they watched the silver disk in its slow descent behind the minaret spire, the curved roof, the balcony where the muezzin stood when calling the hour of prayer. . . .

"Now," whispered the Captain.

Haroun and Nuri slipped into the water and waded to the canalbank. This was where Gaspar had made the crooked footprint not two weeks before. Parting the thick willows, they crept up to the heavy iron-bound water gate.

Haroun pulled the bell rope. Two quick tugs, then one more. . . .

After a long wait, he signaled again.

Soon after there was a muffled clink of chains, and then the thick wooden gate began to rumble upward.

Haroun pulled Nuri into the cover of the willows.

A flaring torch lighted the man inside. "Eh, so you've made another raid!" The man peered out at the canal. "Come in. I can't see you."

A boat glided toward the open gate. The merchant's torchlight gleamed on helmets, chain mail, and scimitars. He yelled in fright and jumped for the chains.

But the boat was already inside. Soldiers leaped out as the other boat came up swiftly to guard the entrance. Haroun could see the soldiers running up stairs and going through doors. Distantly he heard shouts and running.

The doors opened again, and soldiers pushed their captives before them. Soon all the prisoners were huddled together: the merchant, his two helpers who stayed in the house, and the men of his caravan. Some of these had managed to escape through the front door, but later they were brought back by the soldiers stationed at the alley archway.

When the soldiers found a large store of the stolen goods, the Captain sent for Haroun and Nuri. "You mentioned a gold disk, part of the pirate plunder," he said. "Was it like these?" He lifted his hands from a sack, letting disks of gold rain through his fingers.

Haroun examined one. There was the star within the star, the other side blank. He nodded. "Yes, that is like the one we found."

"We have also recovered most of the money the merchant received for the stolen goods he already sold," the

Captain said. "The pirates can't deny their guilt any longer."

It was very late when Haroun and Nuri returned to the Governor's palace with the guards and their prisoners. The boys were led to a chamber where Iskander and the other boatmen were lying fast asleep on embroidered cushions.

But sleep would not come to Haroun and Nuri. Filled with the excitement of their night of adventure and curiosity about the fate of the captives, they tossed restlessly upon the soft pillows.

When footsteps fell on the stone floor, they both sprang up. The door opened and a guard bearing a torch entered. "You're not asleep?" he asked in surprise. "Well, then, awaken your companions, for I have come to take you before the Governor of Samarkand."

The boys quickly roused Iskander and the other men. Hastily tying their turbans and pulling on their best outer garments, they followed the guard through long dark corridors. At last they were led into a great hall, brightly lighted with lamps and hung with silks and tapestries. At the far end the richly robed Governor sat upon fine cushions.

Solemnly the Takshan men walked the length of the hall and salaamed deeply before the Governor.

The ruler of Samarkand gestured toward the rugs before him. "Sit near, my friends, for your bravery and cleverness have made the River Zeravshan safe once more."

As the men settled themselves, Haroun and Nuri respectfully stood back. But the Governor beckoned them forward. "Come close, boys, so that you can tell your part of the story. When the merchant was captured, the pirates saw that silence was useless. Now you and I will fit the whole tale together."

The pirates used to roam the desert, joining passing caravans in the guise of nomads journeying to the cities. At night they robbed the travelers and rode off. In one of the caravans they met Sayyid Ad-Din, who spoke of his new post in the village of Takshan between Samarkand and Bukhara. That night the old scholar died peacefully in his sleep. Instead of robbing the caravan, the brigand chief saw a way of preying upon the rich treasure boats plying the River Zeravshan. Gaspar would take the sayyid's place, for as a boy he used to listen to the scholars debating in Bukhara's parks. Another brigand, who had some hawking experience, suggested they train a kestrel to carry messages between Gaspar and the band.

This plan meant they had to stay in one place a long time instead of riding to some distant city after each attack to dispose of their spoils. In Samarkand the pirate chief found a merchant willing to work with them. The merchant gave Gaspar the rich robes a holy man would wear.

Disguised as an old man, Gaspar arrived in Takshan as Sayyid Ad-Din. On the night he was to release four fishing boats, a terrible storm arose. It was too late to change plans, so when the wind and rain lessened Gaspar made his way to the river and cast off the mooring lines. The rest of the band, waiting on a sandbar in the downpour, succeeded in salvaging the boats as they ran aground. The rain did not quite wash away Gaspar's deep footprints. Haroun, seeing them the next morning, thought they belonged to one of the fishermen. When Haroun found the wedge-shaped footprints again in Samarkand, they seemed familiar to him, though he couldn't remember why. The dent was caused by broken bones which had healed crookedly, though they did not cause Gaspar to limp.

In the role of Sayyid Ad-Din, Gaspar heard all the news and gossip that passed up and down the River Zeravshan. He sent the kestrel on regular flights with word of the treasure boats' movements. Since none of the brigands could read or write, the messages were set down in a code invented by the pirate chief. A downward curve meant "downriver," an upward curve meant "toward Samarkand." Other signs indicated boats, cargoes, and times of sailing.

The pirates struck at night and fled with their plunder, sometimes hiding it in their cave, sometimes taking it directly to the merchant in Samarkand, who sold it for them through his secret caravans. Once after bringing sacks of gold ornaments, the band was surprised at Gaspar's unexpected arrival at the water gate.

Gaspar explained he had come because to refuse the invitation of Sayyid Byram would look suspicious to the villagers of Takshan. Pretending to set out for the real sayyid's mosque, Gaspar had then idled away the afternoon in Samarkand's parks. That night, not knowing the streets in that part of the city, he went along the canalbank to the water gate of the merchant's house. In the morning, the pirates left in the boat in which they had arrived. But

Gaspar, given directions, went through the streets toward the quay. There, he pretended he had just come from Sayyid Byram's mosque.

When the cargo boat stopped at Takshan, Gaspar learned of Iskander's plan to foil the pirates by concealing rich goods among common wares. At once the spy sent the kestrel with a message, releasing the hawk, as usual, from the open roof of the ruined minaret. But instead of flying to the pirate cave, the kestrel was caught in one of the hawk nets in the hills. Gaspar thought the hawk had merely raked away to hunt for food as it had two other times. He was waiting for dusk before going into the hills to find the bird when Haroun and Nuri brought the kestrel to him.

Though badly shaken, Gaspar managed to think of some innocent explanation for the coded message the hawk carried; but the boys still had the clues of the gold disk and the crooked footprint, which Gaspar did not realize he had left behind. Haroun and Nuri also knew of the water gate in Samarkand. Gaspar knew the boys suspected a spy and were determined to expose him. The false scholar had to stop them before they discovered his imposture. When Haroun and Nuri left the mosque, Gaspar added to the message on the kestrel's leg the signs that meant, "Danger. Come quickly."

The following night one of the pirates reached the Takshan mosque on horseback, coming over the high plateau behind the hills. Together, the two men planned the capture of the boys.

Four days later, after Haroun and Nuri showed the supposed Sayyid Ad-Din their hawk traps, Gaspar left the hills, feeling confident that the boys no longer posed a threat to pirate plans. He was stunned to find them aboard Iskander's freighter. Learning of the trap, Gaspar determined to warn his fellow brigands and escape with them. But his plan was thwarted when Haroun, in a desperate effort to protect a holy man, struck and rendered him unconscious.

Gaspar regained his senses as the pirates were fleeing along the riverbank. To help them get away, he tried to lead the Takshan men in the other direction. Then Haroun, aided by the kestrel, exposed Gaspar for the impostor and spy he was.

When the whole story was told, Haroun asked, "What will happen to the pirates and the merchant now?"

The Governor of Samarkand replied, "They will spend many long years repairing the canals and bridges of Samarkand under heavy guard. Their kestrel will be added to my other hawks to be trained for hunting. I have sent my men to their cave to recover their horses and whatever goods they left there. Their plunder or the money gotten in sale from it will be returned to the owners whose boats were attacked. And for the bold men of Takshan, there is a rich reward."

Nuri jumped up and shouted, "Samarkand is truly the golden city!"

12

River Treasure

Haroun stood at the tiller of his father's fishing boat. Nuri, grown taller that past summer, was ready to swing the sail.

Iskander gave the order. "Now!"

The boat swung in smartly toward Takshan. The boys jumped out to haul the craft up on the bank. Yussuf and Mahmud, having landed before them, helped pull on the mooring line.

Haroun said, "It grounded easily. The river is higher now."

Mahmud nodded. "It's because of the rains that began last week. Autumn is well upon us." He and Yussuf went back to their own fishing craft to unload their catch.

Theirs was a brand new boat, as large as the others. The men who had worked freighting cargo on the river that summer had put their wages together to replace the craft Mahmud had lost. When the crewmen returned to their village to fish once more from their own boats, Mahmud and Yussuf could join them.

Haroun, rapidly cleaning fish, said, "Mahmud has changed greatly these last weeks."

Nuri agreed. "He no longer grumbles, and he's not afraid for his garden."

Iskander, overhearing, reminded them, "It was Yussuf's friendship which began the change."

When Mahmud's wife and baby son had died suddenly a few months after he came to Takshan, he had no friend to comfort him in his sorrow. The villagers, not knowing him well, had left him alone. This had made him believe he was not welcome, and it had turned him, through the years, into an unhappy, complaining man whose bitterness had made it even harder for people to like him. His sour disposition had made it easy for Nuri to suspect him of treachery.

"Yussuf knew of the gold amulet Mahmud wore," said Nuri. "He understood, and didn't laugh."

It was an ornament that Mahmud's wife had always worn. He kept it around his neck in memory of her, but he feared that the villagers would laugh if they ever saw him with a woman's ornament, so he kept it hidden.

"It was gold that made me suspect Yussuf was the spy," Haroun admitted, remembering when they had met him coming out of the blue-tiled alleyway.

What Yussuf had hastily concealed in the folds of his waistband had been a gold ornament he had purchased at the home of a goldsmith that very morning. He meant to give it to a young woman of Takshan when he asked her to marry him. She was the servant woman who had been sent with meals for Yussuf when he stayed aboard the cargo boat during the stops at the village. Like Yussuf, she had no family of her own, and this became a bond between them. Now they were married and living with Mahmud, and no one could be more devoted to the older man than his new family.

Iskander took out his knife and bent over a basket of fish to be cleaned. "I can finish this work. You two take the nets home and set them to dry in the sun."

Haroun and Nuri lifted the large heavy basket of wet nets. Together they toiled up the village street toward their house. Ahead of them Mahmud walked beside the limping Yussuf. Just as the two men turned down the side lane to their home, they saw the boys and waved a greeting.

Yussuf had once been a hawker for a rich man in a city far beyond the hills of the Zeravshan valley. A fall from a cliff broke his leg and left him with a limp. Since a hawker must be nimble, he could no longer keep his job. Other employers, fearing that a crippled man could not work hard refused to hire him. Yussuf wandered back to Samarkand, where he had been born, though he no longer had any relatives living there. In this city, by concealing his limp, he found work in Iskander's cargo crew. The motions of the boat excused his awkward steps, and on the overnight visits at Takshan, he usually stayed on board. Only in the wooded hills did Yussuf dare walk freely, not knowing that Iskander measured men in a way different from others. And now it didn't matter if the whole world saw Yussuf limping.

In the yard behind their house, Haroun and Nuri carefully spread out the nets so that the afternoon sun could reach every part evenly. "Hurry," Haroun urged. "There is yet time to visit our traps in the hills."

They paused inside the house to tell their mother where they were going. "Don't be late for the evening meal," she reminded them.

They ran along the canalbank, jumping ditches now swollen with the autumn rains. In the distant fields, men were planting the winter wheat. The place under the big apricot tree was vacant, for old Zena had died near the end of the summer. She was buried by the new scholar shortly after he moved into the Takshan mosque.

The holy man had come at the request of Sayyid Byram, who had heard the story of the pirate spy pretending to be a scholar. Soon the mosque was freshly stuccoed and painted, the house that went with it was repaired, the garden was put in order, and a new roof was built over the minaret. Haroun and Nuri went there once a week with the other village children to learn the Koran.

This evening their traps yielded a fine saker and four half-grown red shaheens. The smaller hawks they let go, but they took the saker back home to set on the perch within the garden shed.

Nuri carefully fed the two black shaheens that they had

taken the previous week. "Tomorrow the cargo boat that takes our hawks to Samarkand will stop here," he said. "Haroun, will you finish the hawk cage tonight?"

"Yes, and it will be the best I've ever made, for Yussuf has shown me a new way to fasten the bars."

Leilah called for them to come and eat.

Their father was already seated. As the rest of the family joined him, Nuri suddenly spoke up. "I don't really care that we didn't get a reward for capturing the pirates. We can work with Father every day in the boat and have him home each night with us."

Gold had been offered to the Takshan men for their brave work that summer night in ridding the River Zeravshan of the pirate menace. But Iskander had asked that it be given instead to the crewmen of the boats that had been attacked. Many of these men, he knew, had been so injured that they could no longer work. "We have our wages," Iskander had said. "And once again we have our own fishing boats."

Now Haroun looked at his family sitting together in the last rays of the sun slanting in through the windows. "The river itself has given us our reward, Nuri."

The real treasure was the peace and pleasure of living and working in the valley of the River Zeravshan.

Rita Ritchie, the author of six successful books for young people, says, "I cannot remember a time when I was not scribbling something." Born in Milwaukee, she majored in zoology at the University of Wisconsin and went on to work as a chemical technician and a research associate for a pharmaceutical company. Throughout high school and college, however, she continued to write, and before she was graduated from high school, she had already had several feature articles published in a suburban newspaper. She also wrote short plays for a children's radio program on a Milwaukee station.

After college, Mrs. Ritchie began to write science-fiction stories, all of which had children in them. The children in these stories were so successful that Mrs. Ritchie soon turned to writing for and about young people. Her historical adventure tales include *The Enemy at the Gate,* about the Turkish siege of Vienna in 1529; *Ice Falcon,* an exciting story set in Iceland at the time of the Vikings; and *Rogue Whaler,* a tale set aboard an American whaling vessel.

Rita Ritchie lives with her husband, Jack, a free-lance writer, in Fort Atkinson, Wisconsin. The couple has three young children.

THE ARTIST

Robin Jacques is well known as an illustrator both in England and in the United States. He spent his childhood in London and its environs, and after completing his education, began a career as a designer. He soon joined an advertising agency, where he remained until the outbreak of World War II.

Mr. Jacques served in the Royal Artillery and Engineers for four years, until he was invalided out of the British Army in 1945. It was during one of his leaves that he met a young publisher, and through him Mr. Jacques began to illustrate many children's books. They include such books as *The Arabian Nights, Gulliver's Travels, A Book of Giants,* and *Black Hearts in Battersea.* Mr. Jacques lives in London.